Mystery Rob
Robson, Sandra J., 1945-
False as the day is long : a
Keegan Shaw mystery

Murder Mystery

Praise for *False as the Day Is Long*—

"*False As The Day Is Long* will take you across the Atlantic, toss you into the London art world, and drag you into the mind of a killer. Sandra Robson has created an appealing protagonist in Keegan Shaw, whose baptism into the world of private investigation pits her against an elegant former hippie who was keeping deadly secrets before Keegan was born. Robson's sleek and evocative prose invites you into an exciting tale you don't want to miss."

—Mary Anna Evans, Benjamin Franklin Award winning
author of the Faye Longchamp archaeological mysteries

"Sandra Robson's *False as the Day is Long* is less about crime than it is about sin. A classic family tragedy disguised as detective fiction, it lures the reader with rich characters and an intricate plot deep into Ross MacDonald territory — where long dead secrets rise from the grave to haunt the living."

—David Housewright, Edgar Award winning
author of *Curse of the Jade Lily*

"*False as the Day is Long* has it all! Keegan is a smart, engaging sleuth with a quick mind and a delightful wit. But beware—there are enough twists and surprises in this fast-moving story to cause sleep deprivation to anyone who starts reading this at night."

—Gillian Roberts, author of the Amanda Pepper mysteries

continued

False as the Day Is Long

A Keegan Shaw Mystery

SANDRA J. ROBSON

Rainbow Books, Inc.
F L O R I D A

Library of Congress Cataloging-In-Publication Data
Robson, Sandra J., 1945-
    False as the day is long : a Keegan Shaw mystery / Sandra J. Robson. --
1st ed.
        p. cm.
    ISBN 978-1-56825-146-2 (trade softcover : alk. paper) -- ISBN 978-1-56825-
147-9 (epub ebook)
    1. Women detectives--Fiction. I. Title.
    PS3618.O3375F35 2012
    813'.6--dc23
                                        2012012466

False as the Day Is Long Copyright © 2013 Sandra J. Robson

Author's Website: www.SandraRobson.com

Softcover ISBN 978-1-56825-146-2
Epub ISBN 978-1-56825-147-9

Published by
Rainbow Books, Inc.
P. O. Box 430
Highland City, FL 33846-0430
Telephone (863) 648-4420
Facsimile (863) 647-5951
RBIbooks@aol.com • RainbowBooksInc.com

Individuals' Orders
Toll-free (800) 431-1579
BookCH.com • Amazon.com • AllBookStores.com

The paper used in this publication meets the minimum requirements of the American National Standard for Information Sciences—Permanence of Paper for Printed Library Materials, ANSI Z39.48-1984.

The cover image is of the Millennium Bridge in London (iStockPhoto.com). The author photo on the back cover is by Cynthia A. Smith.

First edition 2013

17 16 15 14 13   5 4 3 2 1

Printed in the United States of America.

Thanks to Mick, Abby, Nicolas and my flatmates at 146 Finborough Road all those years ago.

To John D. Kennedy, who read and critiqued the first draft of this book while acting as devil's advocate and logician.

And, as always, to my remarkable husband, who always offers to help me with the sex scenes.

Other Books by Sandra J. Robson

Mystery Fiction
  False Impression
Self-Help
  *Girls' Night Out: Changing Your Life
  One Week at a Time*

False as the Day Is Long

Prologue

London, November, 1966

"It's peeing down rain outside," the blonde woman muttered to her companion. "Best have a cab."

The girl behind them hesitated, watched as they joined the depressingly long taxi queue, and opted to walk. If you were already cold and wet through, did more rain matter? She limped out of the tube station in a misery of blistered heels and swollen ankles. Dry clothes and a cup of strong hot tea, milk sloshed in first, the way God intended, were only blocks away. Her spirits rose then dropped as she turned onto Finborough Road and faced the seemingly endless stretch of wet pavement still ahead. By the time she reached No. 146, she was shuffling.

She descended the slippery basement steps with caution, rucksack held over her head, key in one hand. Cold rain slid down the back of her neck as she clicked left, right, left again. Had it locked instead? Not possible. She gave the key another impatient twist, leaned against the heavy door and fumbled her way inside.

The hallway was dim and depressing, but it was dry. At the far end daylight seeped into the lounge through French doors fronting a damp, cheerless garden. The garden was surrounded by a high stone wall and it backed on an ancient cemetery. Sometimes, when it rained for several days, toadstools grew inside on the carpet, as if they were emissaries from the other side of the wall.

She flicked the wall switch, but there was no flash of light.

Damn. Why hadn't somebody replaced the bulb? And who had made the dark smears on the carpet? Something brown and nasty had been tracked halfway to the front door before the tracker doubled back.

The door to the flat's only bedroom was closed. Damn again. If they were already using the bedroom, she wouldn't be able to get her things. She edged past the bedroom door and into the lounge where she halted, stunned by the unholy mess and pungent smell of urine.

The trestle table, where they ate most meals, had been pulled away from the wall and flung on its side. Brushes, tubes of oil paint, coffee cups and an orange plaid tablecloth trailed across the dark red carpet. A paint spattered easel lay on the divan next to a gouged, torn canvas.

Her conscious mind acknowledged the destruction but rejected the body that rested in the midst of it all. The colors were too bright, for one thing, too dazzling for that cold, gloomy room. Coppery hair, blue jeans, dark green Dartmouth sweatshirt, red blood soaking into the large white D. She looked away, through the open door of the tiny kitchen, fastened her gaze on the sink and kept it there.

Ignore the mess, just carry on. It was her own voice, soft, disembodied, muttering a Latin mass. *Fill the kettle with cold water, light the gas ring, scoop tea from the tin into the pot.* Her unwilling eyes returned to the dark red smears and splatters, and moved to the battered face. How much hate had it taken to strike that face until the features were no longer those of a twenty-year-old girl?

The oxygen in the room was evaporating, sucked away by the sour smell of dying. She opened her mouth, failed to breathe, and slid slowly to the floor in a squat. *Like a woman giving birth in a field.* The room tilted and blocked out the light from the French doors. Her body felt weak and oddly empty. No more waiting then, no more chronic fear, no anxious ifs or whens. Who and why were clear. A giggle started in her throat. *The big five, just like senior journalism. Who, what, when, oops! forgot the most important — where and how.* The last two words played a jangly tune in her head. Where could she go now? How fast could she get there? The tune got louder, but she stayed crouched on the floor, eyes fixed on the terrible face. And then she heard the sound, a small rustling noise, as if something could no longer keep still.

The sound came from the bathroom just beyond the kitchen or from the bedroom behind her. That realization, more frightening than a dead body, put a stop to the mindless song in her head.

She put out a hand to raise herself and felt the top of a rucksack. Not hers, she'd dropped her backpack just inside the front door. Her fingers closed over it as the rustling sound increased. She might need it for a weapon. *Back silently out into the hall . . .* The voice was hissing now . . . *Inch past the closed bedroom door, tiptoe up the steps to the street and run up to the ground floor flat.* Edward was always there, writing the great Canadian novel. Edward would let her in and call the police.

She rose slowly, clutching the rucksack, and edged backward. Another noise, this one accompanied by a creak, as if a door were opening.

The careful retreat became headlong flight. She shot down the hallway, tripped over her own backpack and fell against the closed front door. In another second she had flung it open and was flying up cold, slick steps to the street, a heavy canvas bag clutched in each hand, aches, pains and Edward forgotten. Pure panic screamed in her head, a ragged, silent shriek that lasted all the way down Finborough to Old Brompton Road and into the Underground. It continued to fill her ears as she clattered down the escalator and threw herself onto the next train leaving the station.

Chapter 1

Seminole Beach, Florida, 47 years later

I slipped out of my beat-up Top-Siders and waded into the surf. Another morning in paradise: fluffy clouds, no humidity, cobalt blue ocean. The sand looked white and soft enough to pass for an illegal substance and probably had, this being south Florida. I looked up and down the beach. Nowhere did I see a big-haired, bikini-clad blonde with a 42D chest.

There were always plenty of locals around during these best two weeks of the year — after the exodus of snowbirds from up north and the onset of truly hot May weather. Twenty-something mothers huddled under umbrellas with their SPF-coated babies, high school dropouts-in-training sprawled side by side on beach towels, retirees walked their dogs and occasionally each other, up and down the high water mark. There was only one person surf fishing: a redheaded teenager throwing out lines a couple of hundred yards away.

I looked at my watch, 9:20, and started walking in the direction of the inlet. Even if Sunni Russell was a no-show, and apparently she was, you don't waste a morning at the beach.

It was low tide, and the sand was firm and cool on the bottoms of my feet. I passed the redhead, now baiting hooks on two surf rods, and noticed she was considerably older close up. Mid-thirties probably, maybe forties, if she did her own yard work. Instinctively I straightened my spine and flipped blonde hair out of my eyes. I was forty-two myself. Did anybody ever guess me younger from far away?

Probably not.

I watched a pack of surfers floating a few hundred yards out, waiting for anything resembling a big wave. I should be out there too, using my new surf board, not wasting time with a woman I didn't even know. But Tom Roddler had made it a personal request, and my heart still flip-flopped a little when I heard his voice on the phone. Even if he was a serial dater. Even if we had no future together.

Also, to be honest, I was curious about the woman who owned Sol Mates, a dating agency with a self-proclaimed 92 percent success rate.

In her ads, Sunni Russell, clad in a tiny cheetah-skin bikini, not only promised you a perfect life partner, she explained why you were attracting the wrong sort of person and how to stop, stop, stop it. I hadn't had a lot of luck with men lately, and I liked the concept — guaranteed bliss and back-up therapy for one small fee. Actually the fee wasn't small, but I was counting on picking up a few free pointers.

Except she hadn't turned up.

I took a long deep breath of salted ocean breeze and stepped up the pace.

"Hey, are you Keegan?"

I halted and half turned. The redhead with the fishing rods was standing behind me.

"Yes?"

"We're supposed to meet here this morning. I'm Sunni Russell."

"No, you're not." I pushed my sunglasses up on top of my head and eyed her old T-shirt and cut-off, thigh-high jeans. "Too short, wrong color hair . . ." I broke off without saying too flat-chested.

A smile quirked up one corner of her mouth. "Yeah, I am. Amazing what a wig and foam cups will do, huh? You gotta do it, though. In my kind of business, your life's over once you're on the tube. People follow you around, hoping you'll give them advice for free."

"Really?" I shifted my feet in the sand and tried to look like I wasn't one of them.

"Anyway," she lifted a shoulder and let it fall, "it works. I can go to the mall, fish, hang out in sleazy clubs, and nobody notices. And nobody in my condo complex ever connects me with the agency."

"Pretty well kept secret." I couldn't keep the disbelief from my voice.

She grinned and whipped out a Florida driver's license from a back pocket of the tattered jeans.

The picture in the corner, bad lighting and all, was definitely her.

"That's you," I admitted.

"Tom Roddler says you have a gift for smelling out secrets." She collected the license and tucked it away. "More important, he says I can trust you."

"Does he? And does Tom know the real Sunni Russell?"

"Sure, but he knows me as a painter, mostly. I did his house."

That was too weird, even for south Florida. "You own a successful dating agency and you paint houses?"

She flipped up her mirrored dark glasses, her green eyes serious. "Just the insides. I do murals. Tuscan villages, oceans, rain forests. I've painted all over the country. It's my passion, but the agency buys the groceries. I did Tom's foyer on Palm Beach just before Christmas, and we got to know each other." She smiled a little — nice teeth, white and even. "Can we walk a little and talk?"

I shrugged. "Sure."

Sunni piled her fishing gear a foot above the tide line, and we headed down the beach.

"Tom says you're a straightforward kind of person. Here's the deal. My mother's flying to England in a few weeks. She was born there, but she's been in California since she was twenty. The thing is, she hates flying. If there's no train or bus or limo, she doesn't go." She paused and stared hard at the waves frothing in on the sand. "She's up to something, and I want to know what. And don't tell me to ask her; she just changes the subject. My mother's an expert at keeping secrets."

"And this has what to do with me?"

"I want you to travel on the same plane and get to know her. See who she meets and where she goes — and report back. Tom says you're the best when it comes to figuring out stuff."

"You must be kidding," I said, astonished. "I'm no private detective."

"I've had detectives already, two of them, money down the drain. I need a kind of companion."

"I don't do that, either. And even if I did, why would your

mother talk to me? I don't talk to people on planes myself."

"She'll talk if she thinks you're a psychic. She's into them right now. Does everything they tell her. Especially a guy named Steven. He's encouraged her to make this trip."

I was speechless. Almost. "You don't look batty," I said finally, "but you want me to fly to England, tell your mother I'm a psychic, spy on her and report back to you? What made Tom think I'd do something like that?"

"Look, I'm worried. This is more than just unusual behavior. Maybe she's cracking up. Whatever, I need some answers. I've never known who my real dad was or had siblings or anything. If she's going to see some of them — any of them — I want to know it."

"That's what detectives are for."

"I told you, been there, done that. Thousands of dollars worth. My mother's tricky. If she thinks you're following her, she'll lose you in a heartbeat. To throw me off, she keeps telling me she's decided to go to Mexico to an upscale spa for a few weeks. I need somebody who can keep their eyes open and their mouth shut. Especially if there's any trouble."

"What kind of trouble?"

Her mouth slid down at the corners, and she looked suddenly tired. "I don't know. I just know she's got a lot on her mind lately, and sometimes she cries."

"Look," I made my voice a little kinder, "you don't even know me. I may blab secrets to anybody who'll listen."

"Tom says you won't." She folded her arms stubbornly across her chest. "He says you were based in London when you were a photographer, and you know your way around . . ."

"Not anymore. That was over twelve years ago. Things have changed."

She shrugged away my words. "I made up my mind the

first time he mentioned you; I had a feeling about it. Anyway, you've got the right name."

"Excuse me?"

"Steven, my mother's tame psychic. He said she'd meet somebody on the next trip she took who'd help her, like her own personal guardian angel. He said to look for the initial K."

"She told you that, but she won't tell you anything at all about your family?"

She twisted her red hair up in a knot and held it off her neck. "Well, I know a couple of things. My real name is Morning Sunshine Russell. And I was born in a commune."

I sighed. I was about to hear the story of her life. I glanced around for a place to sit and settled on a sun-bleached tree limb the tide had washed in. "A commune? Like a Sixties commune?"

"Exactly like. Near San Francisco." She followed along and sat beside me. "I went out there, and I learned they'd packed up and moved to Colorado. It's still a commune, even after all these years. Very strict, kind of religious. Nobody remembered my mother. Or Gerry."

"Who's Gerry?"

"My stepfather. She thought he was some drugged out loser, but she kind of nursed him back to health, and then she found out he wasn't. A loser, I mean. He came from a northern California family with a ton of money. That's Mom, always falls on her feet. She's an Aries." She glanced sideways at me. "And, no, she didn't tell me all that stuff, Gerry did. He died two years ago — cancer. We talked a lot at the end. He showed me a bunch of old pictures, but he didn't know much about Mom, either. Only that she was English and turned up at the commune after he did."

"She must have a passport."

Sunni shook her head. "Just in her married name — Abby Russell — but her maiden name was Pell. One detective managed to trace her to a farm some place in Lancashire, England, but none of the family had lived there for years. Mom went to London at eighteen, disappeared, and turned up in California a few years later."

The sun was getting warmer. I stood up and pulled off my T-shirt, exposing a bikini top and a lot of mostly tan skin. "Look, I see your problem. But these days I'm just a part-time college teacher with a houseful of renters — mostly temperamental artists — none of whom are getting along at the moment. And I do have a class to finish . . ."

"Hey, it's not a lifetime commitment, it's a free vacation, and she's not going 'til June. A round-trip ticket to London, open return, a nice hotel room, and, say, five hundred dollars in expenses. All you have to do is make friends with my mother and tell me if she sees anybody who might be my father or anything." She looked away. "I was real close to Gerry. Still, there's this huge piece missing for me. I think my birth father was an artist too. I must have got it somewhere."

"Your mother doesn't paint?"

"God, no, not even her own kitchen." Sunni's green eyes were serious. "Look, I've tried to get her to go back lots of times. You know, the mother-daughter thing, show me England? Now all of a sudden she's going secretly, and she's flying. She's sixty-five, she doesn't look it, and I think she's healthy. But what if she's dying or something? I'd not only lose my mother, I'd never find out who my people are." She stopped, swallowed, and plowed on. "Look, I've been married three times . . . I need . . . I just want somebody I can trust to keep an eye on her. What's so wrong with that?"

"There's nothing wrong with it, and you're probably right. I'm just the wrong one to ask, that's all. I can't go around pretending to be psychic. I couldn't keep a straight face."

"But . . ."

"Sorry, there's no way."

Silence. Long silence.

"Okay, I figured it was worth a shot." She gazed out at the ocean, sighed and looked totally lost for about three seconds. Then she flipped down the mirror finish sunglasses, raised one hand in a partial wave and moved quickly back along the beach, defeat showing in every line of her body.

Chapter 2

Five weeks and two days later, I was sitting next to Sunni Russell's mother on a jumbo jet bound for London.

I'd have known she was English without being told, but it wasn't the accent. Forty years of California living had flattened her vowels and modified her sentence structure. What gave her away were word combinations as she chatted with the attendant who delivered our pre-flight champagne; phrases like "mind you" and "messed about," and once when she muttered "peeing down rain" to herself. The last remark seemed slightly tacky for a woman wearing several thousand dollars worth of St. John travel knit, and the St. John itself was startling enough.

Not that I'd expected a little old lady. I mean, sixty is the new forty, right? But to me, an ex-hippie who lived her life according to psychics meant gray, pony-tailed hair, fringed shawls and love beads. Sunni's mother was of a far different species. In fact, in a singles' bar, at night, she'd give you a run for your money. She was model-thin with pale red-gold hair and white skin so fine you wouldn't see wrinkles until the sun hit her full in the face — which wasn't going to happen today.

I stared out my small, rain-splattered window and counted the planes lined up ahead of us. Here I was, strapped into business class, doing what I'd flatly refused to do — spy on somebody I didn't know. Worse, I'd even done my homework and skimmed four pages of notes about Abby and Gerry Russell and their hippie years. It wasn't particularly illuminating, but I had a much clearer picture of daughter Sunni. Who she was and wasn't, I mean.

She wasn't, for instance, the waif-like character I'd met at the beach. Old Sunni had solid steel beams for bone structure. Three days after our meeting she called to see if I'd changed my mind. A week after that she upped the ante another five hundred dollars and sicced Tom Roddler on me.

Tom, a successful state representative, who will run for governor as soon as he sorts out some family problems, is not exactly a friend. Our relationship segues between passionate nights and some memorable afternoons — and actively showing each other the door.

Anyway, Tom flew me to the Bahamas for a long weekend and leaned on me to accept Sunni's offer. His feeling was that I hadn't been in London for years and should go, especially if someone else paid. Mine, unvoiced, was, why did he care? Most likely he and painter-girl had grown close while she was etching Mediterranean pillars on his vestibule, and he was just doing her a favor. Tom had a tendency to do favors for his latest friend.

The thought of Tom and Morning Sunshine and love among the ruins did not keep me from enjoying four days in a private house on Andros Island with him, a full time maid, and a cook who made the best peach soufflé I'd ever tasted. Not to mention the salt water pool, a wine cellar filled with exceptional white burgundy, and some truly earth-moving sex. It bothered me that he wasn't giving me the straight scoop, but Tom had always been an expert at lies of omission.

By the time we flew home, I was considering the English proposition in a new light. If Tom Roddler wanted me out of the way, for whatever reason, the hell with him. It had been a dozen years since I made a living shooting pictures for *Concepts* magazine. Teaching two classes at the college and collecting rent from the people living in my house covered the basics but left little for travel. Why not check out the changes in a city I'd loved on sight and would never see again if I had to pick up the tab? It wasn't as if the artists in my house needed me; they'd argue about rooms and work space and who cooked what and who ate what whether I was present or not. Pretending to be a psychic wasn't such a horrible lie. All you had to do was look vague and murmur, "It is what it is," at intervals. Besides, Sunni's mother lived in faraway California. She'd never know I ratted her out, and even if she did, I'd never see her again.

I called painter-girl and caved. Twenty-four hours later, a travel packet and a round trip business class ticket to London via New York was delivered to my front door. After that it was merely a matter of packing and beating it to JFK to intercept Mrs. Russell as she flew in from Santa Barbara.

And now, here I was, officially on Morning Sunshine's payroll. It was still pouring outside, but our plane was now second in line on the runway. I glanced sideways at Mrs. Russell to see if she was going to flip out when we rolled into first place. At the moment, her eyes were closed, her head was jammed into the headrest hard enough to make a dent, and her fingers were squeezing the life out of an oversized and overpriced Balenciaga bag.

The plane moved forward and turned, there was a rumble that might have been thunder, and we began to shudder and vibrate in place. I heard a sharp intake of breath from the seat next to me as the jet began to taxi, then plunged down the runway, shimmying gently from side to side. Twenty long seconds later we were angling into the sky.

I've never been afraid to fly. Once, when I was covering an Air Force story in Germany, I went up in a military trainer called a Firefly. The pilot did spirals and loop-de-loops and even let me take the controls, until I pulled up too fast and nearly asphyxiated both of us. When they scrapped the Firefly a few months later (because the engines kept conking out at ten thousand feet) I was shooting spring floods in France and shrugged it off as experience gained. You do that at twenty. At forty, you fret more over near-misses.

Even in the current climate, I had no fear of flying, but Sunni's mother had enough for the entire plane. You could almost see terror radiating out of her, and this wasn't even an Airbus. I reached for my camera before I remembered I didn't carry one anymore. Those days were gone too. It had been a long time since a morning without snapping pictures was a morning without meaning.

I relaxed against the headrest, refusing to be infected by the anxiety oozing out of the seat next to me or the lightning outside our window. However, when a sharp jolt shook the plane like God had whacked it with an aggravated hand, thirty-thousand feet above the ground didn't seem like such a hot idea to me, either. Even the flight attendant looked worried, while the pilot maintained total silence in the cockpit. Assuming he was still there.

When it finally calmed down enough for the attendants to unbuckle and move around the cabin, they showered us happily with booze. I'm not a big drinker, and we'd already had our welcome-aboard champagne, but this was a vacation and the drinks were free. I ordered scotch, heard Abby Russell follow suit and was surprised when she turned to me with evident relief and spoke. I never talk to strangers on planes until three minutes before we land.

"I hate takeoffs." Her voice trembled a little as she added water to a glass of dark amber liquid. "And landings. In fact I hate flying, period."

I made sympathetic noises and let my own scotch slide, warm and neat, down my tongue. "Why not go by sea then?" I said finally. "Or skip the whole thing and drive to Mexico or somewhere?"

She shot me a startled glance, took a big gulp of her drink and put the glass down. "Oh, you just have to be patient . . . trust the process . . . my friend Steven says — " she picked up the glass again "— I don't drink usually, hardly anything at all, but I felt I needed something — God, I sound like such a wimp. You don't mind? Flying, I mean."

I shrugged. "It's faster than a boat."

"True. You must be traveling on business then."

"Not really, kind of a vacation."

"I haven't flown in forty years. Once on the way to Luxembourg we had problems all the way." She shuddered. "The intercom kept crackling on in French and German to say it was engine trouble; when they got to English it was just static. We kept coming down and taking off again. Halifax, Reykjavik, Glasgow. It was my first flight anywhere, and it was very worrying."

I smiled at her. "It would worry anybody who wasn't into crashing."

"Oh, I didn't care if the plane went down, not then. I was numb."

Okay. I let that one pass as an attendant arrived with a tray of hot wet wash cloths and a menu for each of us. While we decided on an entrée, she draped our folding trays with white linen cloths and doled out bowls of warmed pecans and bottles of wine. My scotch was barely gone but I poured myself some cabernet anyway. This was nothing like my last flight to England, packed sardine-like into a middle seat with watery Diet Coke and a two-year-old movie.

"I really shouldn't have anything more," she said as she filled her own wine glass to the rim. Then she sipped it down to a fifty percent chance of spilling, gave me a sudden smile that took another ten years off her age and held out a hand. "I'm Abby, Abby Russell."

"Keegan Shaw." We shook.

"Kee — Keegan with a K?"

"Uh-huh. My mother's maiden name."

"It's pretty. Irish." Her eyes drifted away, the same intense green as her daughter's, then back to me. "What do you do, Keegan? I mean, what sort of work?"

There was a longish pause. I made the effort but the word psychic wouldn't roll, fall or even choke off my tongue. "Oh, a little of this and a little of that."

"I used to be quite good at guessing people's occupations." She studied my khaki slacks and jacket. "Something educational?"

I made a mental note to burn all my educator clothes. "I was a photojournalist years ago; now I teach at a small college. Part time."

"And the rest of the time?"

"I have a, well, a kind of rooming house full of artists. That really is a full time job. A cross between reluctant nanny and avenging angel."

An odd look crossed her face, but just then the cabin lights dimmed and a series of jolts shook the plane. We immediately anchored our wine glasses and the chunky man across the aisle, who had risen to his feet, sat down again and snatched at his seat belt.

Abby Russell clamped her jaw and spoke through her teeth. "It'll be all right. It'll be okay. Steven promised . . ."

A legitimate stranger might have asked who Steven was, but I was having trouble with one lie, let alone two. I was, however, beginning to have a great deal of respect for Sunni Russell. Her mother might think she was on a secret mission, but daughter had obviously subverted the tame psychic and probably the travel agent, judging by my strategic seating. The girl knew how to get what she wanted. No wonder she'd been married three times.

When things calmed down again, we got more food. It wasn't fabulous, but Wines of the World accompanied each of the three courses, so that was a moot point. By the time we got to the chocolate mousse, Abby Russell and I were trading boozy life stories.

Well, I was at least. She was one of those people who encouraged you to talk and listened so intently you thought they cared. She said it was wonderful I'd taken up surfing at age 42, admired my tan, and insisted she'd wanted to be a photojournalist since school. She especially envied the nine years I'd spent working abroad. I didn't tell her the work was often boring or that I hadn't touched a camera for three years, not since my husband smashed himself to a pulp driving drunk. When you're downloading your life story on strangers, you stick with the glamour stuff. For a couple of minutes, the Keegan Shaw saga sounded like one helluva life to me too.

I also failed to enlighten her about surfing in the Sunshine State. Unlike California, Florida surfing is a labor of love and ennui. The biggest waves you get off our beaches are two to three feet high, and the ride lasts about 30 seconds, max.

Nonstop conversation seemed to make Sunni's mother calmer. When she ran out of photography and surfing questions, she asked about the artists who lived in my house, and I grew even more expansive. I described the writer, chef, weaver, potter, and Ikebana expert in residence and told funny stories about being a landlady. Most involved broken air conditioning and partial nudity.

"I have a teacher friend, Steven," she said at one point, "who understands artists, the way artists think, I mean, even though he's one himself." She frowned. "That's wrong, too much to drink, I expect. He says everybody gets an opportunity to . . . to make things right. And you have to take advantage of it when it comes, even if it's out of character for you or just terribly hard. He says if you don't grasp that chance, it may be gone forever. Do you think he's right?"

"Absolutely." I was careful not to roll my eyes. After champagne, scotch and wine, I had no idea what I believed and didn't care. Ignorance and apathy: twin answers to all the world's ills.

When the attendant cleared away our dishes, Mrs. Russell ordered a glass of champagne, drank a quarter of it and said suddenly, "That's why I'm making this trip."

She caught me off guard — in the middle of a yawn. "I beg your pardon?"

"To make things right." She gave me a sideways look. "But you — you must know all about that. How karma works, I mean."

"Oh, right." I'd almost forgotten who I was supposed to be.

"I trust him — Steven. You can go to the bank on what he says, but then a friend recommended Carlo, and he was much more specific. I mean, he actually told me what was going to happen, and it always did. Even a flat tire on my car that I got one morning at the gym. But working with Steven was more — comfortable somehow. He said someone I didn't know would be my guardian angel on this trip." Her words slurred a little. "He said to look for the initial K — but just before I left, Carlo gave me both initials — K. S. I'm supposed to rely on that person absolutely."

I hesitated, unable to think of an appropriate response, but I was betting Carlo was a plant and daughter Sunni had been the planter. Or maybe she'd paid both psychics to pass on very specific information to Abby Russell.

Mrs. Russell leaned forward and unzipped a bag on the floor at her feet. "That's why I'm going to — show you something. This is why I'm going to London." She pulled out a wad of newsprint so yellow it was almost pink in the overhead lights. Unfolded, it was the front page of a London paper called the *Evening News and Star*, dated November 24, 1966. A thin red banner identified it as a Late Extra, and the headlines were two inches high:

American Tourist Found Dead In Earls Court.

Chapter 3

I held the creased, brittle paper carefully as I read.

The body of twenty-year-old Susan Miachi was discovered early this afternoon in the basement flat she shared with two flatmates in Finborough Road. Firemen found her body when they were called to put out a blaze in the lounge. The body, though badly burned, showed signs of trauma. Investigations into the death are being led by Detective Superintendent Richard Hartner of Scotland Yard. Anyone who saw a young, red-haired woman hitchhiking between Stratford and Coventry is asked to get in touch with officials.

I handed the newspaper back, and Abby Russell placed it carefully on her tray. "I knew her . . . back then. I was the hitchhiking flatmate. There were three of us, Nigel and me and Susan. And Edward, of course, but he lived upstairs. But I didn't know about — this — until later. Much later."

"Horrible thing," I said.

She shuddered. "It was. Beaten like that."

"Beaten? You had to identify her?"

"Oh, no, the papers got that wrong, I wasn't in Coventry at all. I'd actually taken the boat train to the south of France that morning to meet friends. And they were going on to Greece, and it seemed like a good idea so I went too. London's cold in November, you know. No central heating. Well, not then anyway. And in those days, everybody was travelling around, looking for the next big adventure."

"So, when did you find out about — your friend?"

"Two months later, in Rhodes. Another friend came out to join us."

I glanced at the newspaper on her tray. "Then how did you get that?"

She looked blank. "Oh, the paper? The uh . . . friend. I never had the heart to throw it away. I felt guilty somehow, like if I'd been there, it wouldn't have happened."

"Your friend Steven would probably tell you that's not right."

"Yes, but I didn't do anything, you see. Didn't even go back to the funeral. It was over by then, of course, far too late." Her voice was dreary. "Steven says when you work your way to your center core there are dragons down there. And you have to face them, no matter how old or horrific they are. I don't want to carry that failure with me for the rest of my life."

"But what could you do? After all this time?"

She reached for her champagne. "Find some of the people, talk to them. Something." She drained her glass. "I was a young, very stupid girl in those days, and I made some bad decisions. A couple of them were disastrous. This is my opportunity to make things right. You see?"

I didn't, but I nodded because it was easier. Her chances of finding anyone involved in a 46-year-old death seemed about as likely as me singing backup for Mick Jagger.

Abby Russell couldn't sleep on planes; she told me so. But when they dimmed the lights and lowered the window shades, she tucked herself up with a quilted eiderdown-and-feather pillow anyway. Our seats were like streamlined La-Z-Boys, very roomy, with complicated digital operation pads that shifted your body parts into more comfortable positions at a touch. At its most extended, my seat went almost as flat as a bed.

I pulled up my personal TV screen and checked through the offerings. Movies, documentaries, comedy shows and video games popped up on the menu. I settled for the GPS system, currently tracking us over Greenland, Iceland and the cold blue Atlantic, and adjusted my pillow.

I was just beginning to drop off when Mrs. Russell roused, ordered warmed brandy from a passing attendant, and began discussing her past with herself and, occasionally, with me. Under the influence, she was a dot-dot-dot talker; guilt about her friend Susan Miachi permeated every broken sentence.

". . . too young to die . . . shouldn't have . . . my fault really, didn't like . . . clubs . . . met him at one . . . handsome . . . drove a Porsche . . . didn't believe he was Mafia . . . said . . . he watched . . . all the time . . . mmm . . . she got away . . . but . . . she was scared . . . never got . . . paint again . . . I told her, but she didn't, and she died."

The muttering continued, words running into each other, partial sentences tumbling out, all delivered in a whispery, incoherent jumble: ". . . too trusting . . . brought 'em home to eat when there wasn't any food . . . gave away her clothes . . .

expensive, American stuff . . . husband picked out . . . didn't fit anyway . . . liked Mary Quant . . . anything English . . . Sasson haircuts . . . should been . . . more careful . . . never safe . . .she . . . ran away from him and . . . Earl . . . afraid . . . of Earl most . . . I think . . ." her voice dropped to a disembodied murmur. "Loved . . . clinic . . . so happy . . . far away . . . painting . . . nobody watching . . . but . . . my fault . . . should have . . . known . . . warned her . . . stayed there . . ."

Photographers are known for visual skills, but my strength has always been auditory memory. I found myself filing away Abby Russell's phrases for future reference, while at the same time wishing she'd stop that awful murmuring. After several minutes, she did.

I decided Sunni was right about her mother. Even tanked and chattering, Mrs. Russell told only other people's secrets. I considered inserting a personal question into the monologue like — Where did you hook up with Sunni's father? and What was his name? — to see if she answered automatically, but about that time she opened those green eyes wide and blurted, "Arrested. She said he'd find her . . . kill her when he got out of jail."

I glanced around the cabin at the other passengers, but none of the prone, blanketed bodies stirred.

"I guess he did then," I said quietly.

"No." The word came out with some force behind it. "Steven said no . . . not him . . . not even his friend . . . but . . . she said . . . Earl was a hit man."

"A hit man?" I repeated skeptically.

"Yes . . . but Steven said no. . . but if it wasn't . . . Tony . . . or that Earl . . . then . . . it had to be . . ."

I waited, but she didn't finish the thought. Her eyes were still open, and I could see tears sliding down her face in the light from my TV screen.

"Wait, are you saying you *know* who killed your friend Susan?"

"Yes, no, I don't. I don't." Her eyes squeezed shut. "I have to . . . make it right . . . you'll help . . . help me . . . know what . . . to do . . . Steven said . . ."

Her head dropped back against her pillow and the words became inarticulate noises. When those sounds were replaced by possible snores, I punched the recline arrow on her console, waited 'til her seat moved into full sleep mode and covered her with the eiderdown. Then I burrowed under my own quilted blanket and considered the last, extremely strange fifteen minutes.

When you travel, you hear a lot of stories from strangers. Some are just bullshit and some are absolutely true, told for the relief of dumping on somebody you'll never see again. I had a feeling Abby Russell was drunk and dumping. Too bad her story was incomplete as well as incoherent.

The plane was cold, my buzz had faded, and I was too wired to sleep. I ordered a cup of coffee from a roaming attendant and went through the goodie bag. Ear plugs, hand lotion, eye shade, soft cotton socks. I took off my shoes, pulled on the socks and got out the notes Sunni had mailed me along with her idea of a travel pack: a London transportation pass, a little over 300 pounds in cash and a purple cell phone with international minutes. The phone was a lot cooler than the one I barely used at home. Maybe she'd let me keep it when the job was over. I read through her typewritten notes again, looking for something I might have missed.

What I know about my step father: (From him) Gerald Russell, born 1948, San Diego. Private school. Dropped out of college to join a commune north of San Francisco in October, 1966. Met my mother there in November or

December. Lots of drugs and alcohol so doesn't remember much except that I was born just before Christmas, and it seemed very religious to him. By then, according to him, the summer of love was pretty much finished, the hippies were being infiltrated by nasties, and the commune decided to move to southern Colorado. At that point Gerry and my mom got married, and his trust fund status came to light. He'd been giving his yearly income to the commune. Since he was off drugs, his parents asked him to come back to the city; they credited Mother with getting him straight. They ignored the free love/commune issue and assumed Gerry was my real father, although she gave birth to me two months after she met him. Gerry's parents were killed in a car crash on the Pacific Coast Highway in fog when I was nine and we had even more money. Gerry never really worked, just managed the family money. When he died two years ago, all his assets went to my mother.

What I know about my mother: (From P.I. report) Born Abigail Margaret Pell in Lancashire, England sixty-seven years ago. Went to London at 18 then dropped out of sight. Red-blonde hair, green eyes, size six. Afraid of flying. Dislikes artists and art. (Note: bought me the dating agency six years ago in an attempt to "wean me off my mural painting addiction." [Her words]) Has never mentioned any family member except Gerry and his parents. Ridiculous about having her picture taken. Once sent my father to speak to the editor of a paper that published a picture taken of them at the opera. Started seeing psychics after my stepfather died and has spent thousands of dollars on them. Has been crying a lot lately and recently went to a lawyer about a new will. I'm afraid it's The Big C and she won't tell anybody.

P.S. You have reservations at the Saxon Hotel, Great Russell Street (Central London, Bloomsbury), three blocks from my mother at the Abbott on the same street. I was afraid to put you in her hotel — too coincidental. My cell is 754-8756. Call me every other day or so and tell me how it's going or if you need anything. If I don't answer, *leave a message*. I turn off when I'm painting.

P.P.S: It's critical that you tell Mom you're psychic — that's an instant "in," and I can't think of anything else she'd buy.

P.P.P.S.: I am over forty, undereducated, hyperactive, and live alone in a two bedroom condo in Lake Worth, Florida. I need roots so bad I took back the name Russell, which doesn't even belong to me. If my father is in England, I want to know it. Help me!

P.P.P.P.S. I almost forgot. Here's the only picture Gerry had of him and Mom together.

It was a 4-inch-by-4-inch faded color photograph of a girl in pale red braids and a long, flowered granny dress. She was holding a baby and squinting into the sun. Beside her was a young guy, with a dark beard and mustache, who looked a little like Magnum P.I. "Abby, Morning Sunshine & me, 1967" had been scribbled in pencil on the back of the photo. I slid Sunni's notes in with my own and returned them to my carryall. It was clear to me that daughter Sunni was on the wrong track entirely. She was looking for illegitimacy and lost family. Her mother was looking for — I made a face because the word seemed unreal and melodramatic — *a murderer*.

Chapter 4

The black cab, which was actually canary yellow under its clutter of decal advertising, sped up the Bayswater Road past Hyde Park, circled Marble Arch and joined the crush of traffic that was Oxford Street. The driver, a youngish, lager-lout type, didn't care whether it was my first trip to London or my last and made no attempt to point out the sights. He hunched over his steering wheel, burped occasionally, and growled at traffic.

Welcome back to London.

In the press of clearing customs and collecting luggage, Abby Russell and I got separated. She'd been noticeably cool when the hostess woke us with early morning coffee and crois-sants, and there was a definite lack of eye contact. It could have been hangover, but more likely she was sorry she'd spilled her guts at 34,000 feet and was now pretending she hadn't. It was way too late to tell her what a dedicated psychic I was, so I suggested we meet for dinner or a drink the next day. She said, "Oh, yes, good idea," but we never got around to exchanging hotel information. By the time I dragged my suitcase off the conveyer belt, she'd disappeared through the nothing-to-declare doorway. Which created a problem.

Although I knew exactly where she was staying, I couldn't just turn up without making her suspicious. I'd have to think up a plan — only not now. It was high noon, English time. I'd had less than three hours sleep, and I was fatigued to the point of stupidity.

My taxi swung left onto Tottenham Court Road, then right onto Great Russell Street, and came to a stop in front of the Saxon Hotel. I actually knew the Saxon. I'd once photographed someone there for the magazine, a woman who was supposed to be a modern-day Virginia Wolfe. Her breakthrough novel sank like a stone immediately afterward.

I checked in, dumped my luggage in my room and went back downstairs. For the next twenty minutes, I wandered up and down Great Russell Street, across from Abby Russell's hotel, and wished I'd claimed to be psychic. June in England is always a crap shoot, 51 degrees and rain one day, 91 degrees and wear your shorts the next. At the moment, it was sixty-gray-miserable degrees out, and I'd forgotten how thin Florida jackets actually were.

Bloomsbury hadn't changed radically in the last dozen or so years. The Abbott, once a small residential hotel, was now part of an international chain; but even so, Abby Russell looked more like Ritz or Cadogan material to me. Maybe she just liked being half a block from the British Museum, which hadn't changed at all. It was still gray, still venerable, still looming. Then I saw the spectacular new glass roof and remembered that the Central Great Court had been cleared out completely since my last visit with only the Museum Reading Room left intact.

The damp, insidious cold was too much; I bought a London map at a small shop and ducked into a café to warm up. It was across from Mrs. Russell's hotel and was one of three places Karl Marx supposedly hung out while writing *Das Kapital* (the other two being the Museum Reading Room and the local pub). It was now a Tudor repro with white painted plaster walls, black wainscoting, black chairs and newsprint top tables. I ordered a pot of real English tea and sat at the window where a fish and chips sign printed in four languages partly blocked my view. While I waited, I looked up Finborough Road on the map, the street where Abby Russell's friend Susan Miachi had met her fiery end. Finborough Road was located in the Earls Court area, S.W. 5, but that didn't tell me much. In my day, Earls Court was just an Australian-Canadian suburb, known for cheap food and low rent.

The tea was strong, hot and milky, and I'd downed nearly all of it when Mrs. Russell descended the steps of her hotel and headed west toward Tottenham Court Road. I folded up my map, dropped two pound coins on the counter and shot out the door to follow her.

The smell of car exhaust was thick on Tottenham Court Road. I breathed in with a sense of nostalgia. Forget emission controls; if London had a signature perfume it would forever be *eau de hydrocarbon*.

I caught Mrs. Russell up at the tube station and followed her down the monster escalator into the Underground where she took the tunnel leading to the Northern Line. She didn't hesitate or seem unsure of herself like somebody who'd been away for forty-plus years, but the place probably didn't look all that different. Maybe a little fresh paint. There were a lot of people moving around. Still, it was easy to keep track of her celery green raincoat in the midst of all that brown and gray and working navy.

I stayed back behind little groups of people on the southbound platform. Her eyes were fixed on the railway tunnel, which suited me fine; she apparently knew how to lose trailers at will.

When the train came I boarded the car next to hers and stood by the sliding doors, watching at every stop. At Charing Cross Road she switched to the District Line and rode six more stops. By then I was pretty sure where she was headed and didn't worry so much about losing her.

At Earls Court I inserted my transportation pass in the exit machine and watched with relief as it popped up on the other side. Then I trailed Mrs. Russell to Finborough Road.

Apparently she was returning to the scene of the crime.

By the time she paused in front of 146, I was on the opposite side of the street, screened by a constant rush of traffic, feeling smug. I'd never followed anybody in my life, but I could have jogged circles around her in a gorilla suit, and she wouldn't have noticed.

The building where Mrs. Russell had lived with her flatmates in the sixties looked like the other three-story terrace houses on Finborough Road. Same brick structure, same stone trim, same lower bay window. Even the doors were mostly painted black. Number 146 looked a little seedier than its neighbors, paint peeling, bricks faded and dirty, unwashed curtains sagging in the windows.

Abby Russell climbed the steps to the ground floor flat, avoided an overturned dust bin and rang the bell. When nobody answered, she returned to the sidewalk and looked through black iron railings into the basement area. The gate to the basement stairs was ajar, and I expected her to go down and ring that bell too. Instead she drew her shoulders up, turned and walked straight back to the Earls Court tube station. There she took the District Line to Sloane Square, exited and headed down the King's Road.

The King's Road is Chelsea's main street. Its shops were not as up-market as the ones in Sloane Square. Some of the small boutiques I remembered had been replaced by chain stores, but it still had the look and smell of trendy. After all, it was the cradle of New Age civilization — the birthplace of both miniskirt and punk rock. I stayed behind a woman dragging a corgi dog on a pink leash and kept one eye on Mrs. Russell and the other on the windows of Peter Jones Department Store.

Five or six streets down, just past a restaurant called The Alibi (where I once had a six hour lunch with an impoverished but great looking Viscount), Abby Russell took a right, walked another block and stopped in front of a double storefront painted navy blue. The gold lettering on its display windows read:

Josef's at Jubilee Walk, Opened 1965.

Mrs. Russell was apparently interested in a poster in one corner of the window. She stood there long enough to learn it by heart, then back-tracked slowly to the King's Road. I ducked into a shop that sold only black T-shirts and waited.

She passed the T-shirt window and continued walking in a distracted manner, but given her age and the amount of alcohol she'd consumed on the plane, it was a miracle she was upright.

I tagged along, hanging back, trying to think of a way for us to meet. Bumping into her on the street, or boarding the same train in the Underground or hanging around her hotel pretending to be visiting the British Museum were all bad ideas. London is known as a city where you never see the same cab driver twice. On the other hand, maybe Mrs. Russell didn't know that. She'd been away over 40 years.

I was still thinking when Sunni's mother stopped suddenly in front of the Habitat store, shook her head and stepped out in the street to hail a taxi. One swerved over immediately, she hopped in, and off they went, leaving me and my partially open mouth on the sidewalk. Or pavement, as the Brits persist in calling it.

It was several minutes before I found a taxi of my own, an agonizingly slow one, and told the driver the Abbott Hotel. Once there I asked the girl at the desk to buzz Mrs. Russell's room, but there was no answer. Then I sat in the lobby for an hour, waiting to see if she turned up.

Of course, she didn't. She could have been anywhere, with anyone, like Sunni's birth father or the entire Manchester United football club.

I was weary, bummed and totally out of ideas. Visions of crisp white sheets and soft mattresses popped up before me like surreal TV ads, but it was too late for sleep. The only real way to deal with jet lag is to crash for two hours on arrival, then get up and stay up, zombie-like, until bedtime. It's a balls-to-the-wall approach, but you wake up the next morning on Brit-time. If I gave in and slept now, it would be days before I got straight.

I decided to do a little exploring instead, have a half pint of ale in some warm pub — emphasis on warm — and pick up Mrs. Russell later. I cut down Museum Street, crossed High Holborn to Drury Lane and walked toward the Thames.

The farther I walked, the better I felt. As Ben Johnson once said, "It's hard to stay aggravated in London." Well, what he actually said, "When a man is tired of London, he is tired of life," but why quibble over semantics.

London has been my city since age nine when I found a 1954 Souvenir London Picture Book in my aunt's attic. There were no colored pictures in its entire twenty-eight pages. The Crown Jewels, Piccadilly, St. Paul's, the Houses of Parliament, The Tower, even Westminster Abbey — all came in tasteful shades of white and gray. That summer I learned the name of every building, bridge and statue by heart. When I finally made it to England years later, it was like Ted Turner had colorized the city. The Thames was brilliantly blue, the Houses of Parliament reflected gold in the afternoon sun, and bright scarlet buses accessorized every street corner.

The next day the temperature dropped, and it rained for two weeks straight. I didn't care. London was my one and only case of love at first sight, and that never changed. Not even when I traded it for Florida and a man I confused with my destiny.

When I reached the Strand, I turned down Fleet Street to wallow in a little nostalgia. After wandering up and down a few side streets, I found the offices of my old employer, *Concepts* magazine, but they had been taken over by lawyers, or rather, barristers. Worse than that, the pub we'd frequented nearby — crackling fire, overstuffed chairs, half pints of ale — was now a wine bar with harsh lighting, weird colors and metal chairs.

Depressed, I turned away, dodging tourists, and nearly tripped over a blonde with Jackie O sunglasses and several large Harrods' shopping bags. We disentangled, muttered, "Sorry," at each other, and I abandoned Fleet Street for a landmark you could count on — Trafalgar Square.

The old double-decker buses, the kind with open platforms at the rear, were mostly gone, thanks to an American lawyer who fell while jumping off one and took it personally. The new buses were like those in any major city. I flashed my transportation pass and felt decidedly surly. Someone had made a lot of changes since I lived here and not once had they consulted me.

Trafalgar Square was, at first glance, the same. Fewer pigeons, of course, since the Town Council decided they were pests and imported trained falcons to thin their numbers. And the street in front of the National Gallery was now a pedestrian walkway. But the huge bronze lions guarding Nelson's Column were still solidly in place. You don't take out lions cast from French cannon with a few testy falcons.

I stood for a moment where crowds of Londoners once gathered to hear Churchill say the war was over, and I watched the fountains glitter in the sunlight. Then I cut through the pedestrian traffic to the statue of Edith Cavell.

Nurse Cavell was famous for smuggling downed British fliers out of German-occupied Belgium during WWII. I knew the quote at her bronzed feet by heart: "Patriotism is not enough. I must have no hatred or bitterness toward anyone." The words always gave me a rush — particularly since she uttered them twenty minutes before she was shot for treason. Today, for some reason, the rush never materialized. I stood there for a long time, remembering things that had happened during the last few years, and the people they had happened to, without feeling much of anything. After a while, it started to rain.

Tourists began to run for cover; umbrellas popped up everywhere. I jogged up Charing Cross Road, detouring around a woman with blonde hair and a ton of shopping bags. All the cabs were taken. So, I slogged on through the downpour, hoping for a real pub without real hope. Twelve years was a long time. Why had I remembered soggy shoes and wet gray days with such longing and regret? Better to be home right now, balanced on my board, skimming waves. Wiping out and being tumbled through warm, foamy seawater was far preferable to this. Hell, listening to my squabbling tenants at home was preferable to this. The truth was, I had talked myself into a job I wasn't qualified to do, and the reward was a depressing reminder that the past is never where you remember putting it.

I walked another spirit-drenching block. Quitting would mean refunding Sunni Russell's money. I could live with that. It wouldn't be the first time I'd been in hock to my credit card.

As I turned down Great Russell Street, I was nearly bowled over by two sleazy looking guys walking on the wrong side of the sidewalk. The way they stopped and looked after me was unsettling. I'd always felt safe in Bloomsbury, in fact, in most of London. You just watched out for pickpockets and reported any packages left in tube stations by guys with Irish accents. I walked a little faster. In retrospect, the IRA seemed almost benign; they'd blown themselves up as often as anyone else.

Back at the hotel, I ordered tea up to the room and stripped off my saturated clothes. I was draping them across a wing backed chair when I looked out the window and saw someone I recognized. It was the blonde from Fleet Street, the one in Jackie O sunglasses with the Harrods' shopping bags. In fact, I'd brushed past her on Charing Cross Road too, now that I thought about it. She was standing across the street, watching my hotel, from under a black umbrella.

It was a couple of seconds before I actually got it. I'd followed Abby Russell around this afternoon, smug at how oblivious she was to my presence. Now somebody had returned the favor, only she'd done it better; she hadn't lost me. A truly pathetic example of the blonde leading the blonde.

As I watched, the woman turned and went down the street toward the British Museum. There was something about the way she moved — short, stiff steps — that reminded me of a man trying out high heels.

I shook my head in disgust. Obviously I'd picked up some weirdo wandering around town and now she — or he — knew where I lived. It was absolutely time to go home, and I'd only been here about fifteen minutes.

There's nothing lonlier than a hotel room with only you in it. I reached for my purse, extracted the new phone and rang up Tom Roddler. He wasn't in, surprise, surprise. I left a brief message. "Hi, I'm in London," followed by my cell phone number. Then I wrapped my wet hair in a towel and curled into the fetal position on top of the bed. It was time to face a few hard facts.

The London I'd seen today was Americanized to an alarming degree — fast food on every corner, cell phones pressed to every ear, black cabs now red and pink and yellow and decorated like NASCAR racers.

My London had been thoroughly English, traditional and frequently quirky. I liked the way Brits drove on the left side of the street, forcing you to look the wrong direction at crosswalks or risk annihilation. I liked how they showed you their gardens with pride, even if they were only two by two plots. I didn't even mind that they loved their dogs as much as their spouses.

London, London, you were perfect years ago. Stop changing.

Chapter 5

E leven hours of sleep will cure just about everything — from zits and fine wrinkles to a temporary loss of backbone.

I woke the next morning to full sunshine, room service coffee and renewed confidence. Today I would find a way to reconnect with Abby Russell, even if I had to play the dreaded psychic card. Today Abby Russell would not lose me, no matter how erratic her behavior.

I showered, dressed, went down to Karl's Café and commandeered the seat in the window. I was reading the *Times* for news, and the *Daily Mirror* for intellectual balance, when I noted Mrs. Russell coming out of the Abbott Hotel. She hopped into a waiting taxi and high-tailed it out of Bloomsbury.

Well, shit.

Sunni's mother must have spotted me yesterday and wasn't

taking chances. So much for self-confidence. And never mind that today was report-in day. I considered my dwindling lack of options then pulled the purple cell phone out of my jeans pocket and thumbed in Sunni's number. Better just get it over.

It rang only twice before her voice said to leave a message, and I remembered she turned off when she was working. Then it came to me: It was four in the morning on Palm Beach. So, what if she wasn't working all night transforming somebody's utility room into the Taj Majal? What if she was busy turning Tom Roddler into a quivering mass of jelly? Was that why he wasn't answering calls?

I closed my eyes and got a grip. I was several thousand miles away. Tom was always going to be Tom. Besides, he'd wanted me out of town, the hell with him. As for Sunni, if I couldn't reach her, then I didn't have to admit losing her mother twice in as many days.

"Just reporting in," I told the phone. "It's about nine-thirty Thursday morning. Yesterday your mom went to a flat at 146 Finborough Road in southwest London where she used to live. A friend of hers died in a fire there in 1966, and it's apparently bothering her. Then she went to an art gallery called Josef's of Jubilee Walk in Chelsea. Hasn't talked to anybody in particular as far as I know. Nothing else of interest except some creep in drag followed me around town yesterday afternoon. I'll make sure he doesn't do it today. More later."

I ordered still another cup of coffee and revisited my options. The flat in Finborough Road had to be a dead end after forty years, and that left only one possibility. I folded my newspapers and went to check out that possibility.

Josef's of Jubilee Walk, all dark blue paint and gold trim, had a rich, polished look in the 10:00 a.m. sunshine. I studied the poster in the window, the one that had so engrossed Mrs. Russell. No wonder it had taken a long time to read; the words were nearly obliterated by slashes of hyperactive color:

OPENING: *The Vengeance of Fusion.*
Meet the artist Beijing. Friday 23 June, 6:00–9:00.
Public invited. Exhibit continues through August.

As I deciphered slashes, a kid carrying a heavy looking, plastic-covered object walked past, booted open the front door and went inside. After a couple of seconds, I followed.

The gallery's front rooms were spare and elegant with shiny, light wood floors, white molded walls and a number of cream painted hallways leading somewhere else. None of the widely spaced paintings were attributed to anyone named Beijing. There was no one covering the reception desk, and when nobody came to see if I wanted anything, I went exploring.

The hallway to the left dead-ended in two exhibits. One, titled, The Real America, was composed of giant black and white photographs with subway graffiti scrawled in red magic marker across them. The pictures were mostly of abandoned pickup trucks with West Virginia license plates. The most interesting graffiti read:

Hooray, hooray, the first of May,
outdoor fucking starts today.

The second exhibit, Erin the Free, consisted of sections of real green grass sod, a computer circuit board and a battery. Wires were attached from the battery to the grass with Play Doh and every twenty seconds or so, a red bulb lit up and sparks flew out into the grass.

Beijing's name was scrawled enthusiastically over both of these works of art.

I ducked down another passage and emerged into a no-man's land of sculptures, carved stones, paintings and tall, skinny wooden figures. In one corner of this great-room a girl with long, bronzy-red hair was having a fit. Her hair, thick and spiky at the same time, looked as if she'd bent over as far as she could and cut upside down into whatever bits fell forward.

"I want the freaking cross to stand alone," she was hissing at the kid I'd followed inside. "Can't you understand the concept, damn it! If it's too close to The Tree of Life, it loses all impact."

The kid shifted the heavy piece he was holding and was immediately screamed down. "Not there, you twit!"

There was more hissing and swearing before a distinguished man with gray-streaked hair entered, crossed the room and grasped her arm. "Beijing, darling. Please stop." He smiled the whole time, pretending she wasn't trying to shrug him off. "Placement is my job. Mine and Nigel's. We'll take good care of everything. Come in the back for a cuppa and relax a little."

"Piss off! I don't want any fucking tea. I hate tea."

"Dmitri," he shot a look at the kid, "a latte from down the road, please."

Ignoring her protests, the man edged the girl away from the cross and into a back room. When the door closed behind them Dmitri let out his breath, propped his burden atop a white pillar with no particular care and saw me standing behind him.

"Are you in charge here?" I said. "I had a question about the opening tonight."

He pushed a hand through magenta and black hair. "No, God, no. I — I have to —" He brushed past me and fled down the nearest hallway.

I went over to look at the cross.

It wasn't my kind of art, but I was brought up Southern Baptist and never got over it. The cross was formed of large pieces of broken mirror rising out of a work-calloused hand. A nasty looking nail stuck out of the palm and sins had been etched on the mirror pieces in red. There were so many sins the artist had nearly run out of cross: gossip, drunkenness, gluttony, murder, etc.

"I'm afraid we're not really open. Can I help at all?"

I had watched the guy approach in a fragment of mirror labeled sodomy, so neither his presence or voice was a surprise. I put a smile on my face and ignored his faintly hostile look. "As a matter of fact, you can. Is this for sale?"

"Ah." Caution replaced hostility. He wanted to throw me out, but the American accent might mean I had more money than I looked. And with the present economy . . .

"Well, actually, it's one of the pieces being shown tonight. From the artist Beijing." His bottom lip tightened a little on the name.

"Oh, yes, I just saw her." The literal truth, anyway.

"Did you? Well, I'm afraid we're not equipped to preview . . ."

I stopped listening to the explanation because he didn't fit his voice in any way. To match the supercilious tone and constipated expression, he should be wearing a pinstriped suit and toting a rolled umbrella. Instead he had curling hair, a three day beard, baggy black pants and a baseball cap. He looked like a young rocker.

I waved a hand at the cross and interrupted. "Not a problem, I'll just come back tonight. For the opening."

"Yes, of course. We'll be delighted to see you. Much better tonight — things are a bit — ah — messed about."

I smiled, nodded and went back the way I'd come in, down the hallway, past Real America and Erin the Free and out the front door. Only after I closed it behind me and heard a delayed click did I realize he'd tagged along to lock up. I turned to look and met his eyes through one of the small window panes. For a couple of very long seconds we stared at each other, then he blinked and gave me a smile that said he was accustomed to that kind of attention and appreciated it.

I turned away thinking, *What a jerk!* A hot looking jerk — he obviously thought so — but not really good looking enough to get away with that kind of crap. Just one of those hair and glare boys: big attitude, minimal charm.

I walked back to the tube station, watching for a place to pick up some paperbacks. I had a plan for tonight, but it involved a couple of assumptions. One was that Abby Russell spent so much time reading the gallery's opening poster because she meant to attend. Two was that by 6:00 tonight I could think up a lie good enough to explain what I was doing there when she turned up.

If neither of those assumptions was correct, I would need the paperbacks. Based on the art work I'd seen so far, it was going to be a very long evening.

Chapter 6

At 6:45 that evening the sidewalk outside Josef's at Jubilee Walk was standing room only. I edged around a skin head in a sarong, a girl in motorcycle leathers and two guys who looked like they'd come straight from the office. All four were chatting up a Liz Hurley look-alike in a bikini top and feather skirt.

There were even more people inside the gallery, and I stuck with them; it was 58 degrees outside, and my little black dress, which was actually dark green, didn't cover a lot. Armed with a plastic glass of mediocre red wine, I followed the large, frantically colored signs that pointed the way to Beijing's showroom and mingled enough to see that Abby Russell hadn't yet arrived.

The show room was a paean to order compared to the way it had looked that morning. The Mirrored Cross and The Tree of Life were getting a big play from a cadre of people, dressed in black-on-black, who were oohing and aahing in art-speak. Another group of art lovers was clustered around a six-by-five-foot canvas, discussing what the artist meant. On closer inspection, I understood why. The painting was regulation seascape until you got within a few yards: green-blue sea, white fluffy clouds and a girl wading through dense, foaming waves. The girl had tanned arms and legs, a blue dress, a swan-like neck and no head. The neck simply faded up toward a suggested lower face, which in turn faded to blue sky. Two other paintings were missing heads too.

I couldn't decide if Beijing had trouble with faces or if it was just way too deep for me. The crowd clearly suspected the latter as phrases like "woman-child-imagination" and "conventional-emptiness" laced the culturally charged air. Only one man dissented, sneering, "Derivative," and insisting Bill Brandt did it better and first. Whoever Bill Brandt was.

The only person I recognized in the entire place was the coffee-gofer Dmitri, who was circulating among groups of people. Nowhere did I see Beijing or her distinguished looking keeper or even the arrogant guy with the curly hair and sex-in-a-thicket look. Not that I was looking for him. I worked my way back to the front room, parked near a window and watched for Mrs. Russell.

Sunni had returned my call earlier in the afternoon, apologized for missing me, and said she'd been painting all night — alone. The fact that she hadn't been with Tom gave me such a rush of relief, I immediately confessed my failure to play the psychic card and shadow her mother efficiently. She wasn't as upset as I expected, but she was bowled over by the fact her mother had gone to an art gallery. She agreed that attending the opening was a smart move, and I could hear the hopeful note in her voice; maybe I'd stumble across her father while I was there. She told me to give her a heads up any time, day or night, and she'd be on the next plane to London.

It was after eight o'clock when Abby Russell finally turned up. She was wearing a swingy tweed jacket and Chanel ankle boots and her red-gold hair spiked expensively around her face. She moved quickly through the crowd to the show room, which was now solid with bodies, then made a slow circuit, studying each offering. She shrugged off most of them, including The Cross and The Tree of Life, and finished up at the three headless paintings.

I hadn't expected her to like those, either, and I was surprised when she stayed glued to them. It was probably six full minutes before she backed away, turned, and stared around the room, face grim, green eyes more than troubled. She hadn't noticed me standing a couple of feet away, but she soon would. I decided to speak first and use my prepared lie while the lying was good. I practiced under my breath:

"One of the artists at my house told me to be sure to see this exhibit while I was in London. Beijing's work is supposed to be . . ."

I took a deep breath, lines memorized, and reached out to tap her on the shoulder. At that moment, the noise level rose, the crowd parted behind us like the Red Sea, and Mrs. Russell and I turned at the same time to see what was causing the fuss.

The gray haired man I'd seen that morning appeared like royalty in the cleared path with the artist Beijing on his arm. She wore a forest green dress with sleeves to her fingertips and a neckline open to her bellybutton. An ornate letter B in lacy white metal hung down between her breasts. It could have been a D or even a C with all the curlicues, but I was betting on B. Her skirt ended just slightly lower than her personal parts and just slightly higher than the lacings of her clear plastic platform shoes. Kind of a Sharon Stone does-the-arts look.

Abby Russell was staring at the man, taking in every detail of his hair, face and European cut suit. Then she shifted her attention to the girl. Her back went ramrod straight — and she folded neatly into a pile on the floor.

I was the only one who noticed, at first, since everybody else was ogling the artist. Then Dmitri, the gofer, erupted out of the crowd. He helped me get Sunni's mother to her feet, and a girl with very white make-up and long blonde hair retrieved Abby's purse and handed it to me. Dmitri and I were struggling to keep Mrs. Russell upright when Beijing's companion moved through the crowd to offer help. Up close he looked like an investment banker.

"Would she like to rest in back?" He waved a hand at a paneled door in the back of the room. "Can she walk that far?"

Abby's eyes opened briefly. She twisted her head around and saw me.

"Thank God!" Her fingers closed over my wrist. "For God's sake, don't leave me."

Three men were hanging out in the back room. One was the sneering rocker boy I'd met that morning and the other two were considerably older. All of them looked surprised as Dmitri and I edged Abby Russell through the door and onto a metal folding chair. One of the older guys had thick silver hair, noticeably blue eyes and a camera around his neck. The other had high cheekbones, chemically engineered blonde hair and a vintage red leisure suit. I blinked my eyes at the little gold tail on a chain around his neck. Somewhere there was a disco ball twirling around without an owner.

Dmitri faded away before I could thank him, and disco boy snatched up a magazine and fanned the air in front of Abby's face.

Sunni's mother was a nasty gray color, and she was breathing like an asthmatic, but she pulled her chin back from the breeze and managed to raise a hand. "Stop. Please."

"Certainly, dear lady, certainly. Are you recovered?"

She nodded, breathed in through her nose a few times and stared back at him. Then, "You're Nigel, aren't you? Nigel Cunningham?"

"I am." He grinned at her. "Have we met?"

She took another slow breath and nodded. "One forty-six Finborough Road. It's Abby, Nigel."

His face went blank, then disbelieving. "Abby . . . Abby Pell? Not true." He hesitated, stuttered, and made a theatrical gesture at the blue-eyed man with the camera. "But, but here's Edward — you remember Edward? He's reviewing this — I hesitate to use the word — show. Vengeance of Fusion, I mean to say!" Nigel's face split in a malicious grin as he turned to the gray haired banker type. "And you knew Josef at once, of course. You must be psychic, darling. You turn up after a hundred years — and the gang's all here!"

Abby Russell's eyes squeezed shut, and I thought she was headed for the floor a second time. Her grip on my arm involved fingernails and was painful.

Josef had yet to speak. He looked distinguished, kind, and slightly puffy, but his dark eyes were those of a younger, warier man. His lips moved, forming words and discarding them, until he was saved by a voice from the open doorway.

"Josef! Are you helping me or not?" The plea was angry, mildly frantic, and accompanied by a huge shake of red-brown hair and flashing eyes.

"Of course, of course." He swung around, saw people staring through the open door behind Beijing, and lowered his voice. "I'll be along soon."

"Now, Josef," she hissed at him.

"Yes, all right. Yes." He turned to look at Abby. "I . . . what a surprise, Abby, I hardly know what to say. You're looking well. Very well. I . . ." His hand described a half moon toward the furious girl in the doorway. He took a step backward. "I'll talk to you later, shall I? When the opening's over. Wonderful to see you." He went, closing the door behind him.

"He's lovely, Josef, isn't he? Never changes." Nigel rolled his eyes. "Nor does Beijing. I wonder, do they call her Beige, for short?" He looked down at Abby. "Better now? Like a drink of something? All right now?"

Edward fetched a plastic glass of brown colored liquid and offered it to her. She shook her head. He insisted, holding it steady until she sipped at it several times. My wrist began to burn, and I shifted it a little.

"I'm so sorry." Abby glanced down at her fingers and let me go. "I didn't realize . . ."

Everyone in the room seemed to be listening and waiting. Edward and Nigel exchanged an expressionless glance and the young, curly haired guy wasn't sneering any more. He looked from Abby to me and back again in an assessing manner. If he mentioned seeing me at the gallery earlier in the day, what should I say? His eyes met mine and, after a second, I saw him decide to let it go.

"This is Josef's son, Reid," Nigel said suddenly, waving a hand at the kid. "Haven't I said? He's the gallery's right hand man and heir apparent of," his palm indicated the back room, "all this."

Abby sat up straighter with an air of retrieving her manners. "My friend, Keegan," she murmured at me, "Keegan Shaw.

We flew over together from New York yesterday — no, the day before."

Nigel put out a hand, shook mine. "Nigel Cunningham. Edward Mowery, Reid Kardos," he said, indicating the other two men. "Well, that explains your near-faint," he said brightly. "Jet lag, I expect. And low blood sugar. You always had that, didn't you?"

"Fancy your remembering." She gave him a small smile. "Except for your hair, you haven't changed all that much."

The corner of his mouth turned up. "Thank you, darling. You have, though. Quite a lot, actually. Still a fashion plate, I see, but your hair's lighter and you've acquired an American accent." He made a face. "Or is that mid-Atlantic?"

Her voice was firmer than her smile. "My friends think I sound very English."

He reached out and patted her shoulder. "My God, this calls for a celebration. Let's go someplace for dinner and catch up." He turned to look at Edward. "You've got all the pictures you need, yes? As the Americans used to say, when asked, 'Let's blow this joint.' "

"Oh, no, I wouldn't want . . ." Abby began to protest.

What she didn't want got lost in Nigel's surge of enthusiasm. "Not at all, not at all. We've been sitting round trying to think up an excuse since we arrived. We're dying to get out of Dodge. Join us. And, of course, your friend." He turned his attention to me. "Americano, correct?"

"Last time I looked."

His left eyebrow went up; he grinned at me. "And are you an American now too, darling? Last time you looked?" This to Abby.

"Californian, actually."

He all but rubbed his hands together. "Wonderful. Well enough to move now? A little food and you'll be right again.

Can you arrange a taxi, Edward? My car is, unfortunately, in use. We'll play catch up with Josef later. I'm sure he'll be occupied until the wee hours. Reid?" He turned to the younger man. "Come out for a nosh?"

"Better not — better stick here." Reid gave Abby Russell a slow measuring look, then shifted it intact to me. "Nice to have met you."

Nigel opened the door and herded us out.

There was an even bigger crowd in front of the gallery than before, but it was a polite mob, and they shifted to let us through. Edward was looking for a taxi when Abby realized she didn't have her purse. I volunteered to go for it, she said no, she'd get it, then yes, then no again. I hustled back inside while she was working it out.

Dmitri, the gofer, was in a near-lascivious huddle with the blonde in the long white dress just inside the front door, but neither Reid nor Josef nor Beijing were anywhere in sight. I hoped they hadn't left gofer boy in charge; his attention was definitely not on the crowd. I found the purse in the back room. Somebody had apparently kicked it into a corner.

While I was searching for it, somebody pushed Abby Russell in front of a cab. At least that's what she said when I arrived with her bag. The art crowd had spilled off the sidewalk into the street, several vehicles had jammed to a stop and stayed there, and an angry cab driver was gesturing frantically in a language no one understood. He kept pointing to the light on his roof and the two clients in the back seat. "Occupi — occupi — jump — oot ."

"What happened?" I came up behind Edward, who was busy keeping Abby Russell on her feet.

"She thinks she was pushed . . ."

"I was pushed!" Abby hands were shaking. "Somebody

shoved me off the curb right into the street just as the taxi came. It nearly hit me!"

"Well, not quite," Edward soothed. "He was quite a way off, really. I expect the crowd was jostling a bit, not paying attention . . ."

"Darling, what's all this?" Nigel joined us at the curb. "I stop in the little boys for half a sec, and the whole place goes up in smoke?"

"Somebody pushed Abby in front of a car," Edward said.

Although the two men did not look at each other, their expressions were identical — disbelief. But not, interestingly enough, the kind of disbelief that said their long lost California friend was a blithering paranoid.

"Well," Nigel looked around for a second, then blinked at her, "this is London. It does happen." He raised an arm and an unoccupied cab inched toward us. "Shall we?"

Abby flashed a look at the curious crowd, standing around and soaking up yet another drama involving her. "I don't know. I guess. Yes, now, please."

She jumped in the cab, and I followed, still carrying her purse.

Chapter 7

The restaurant Nigel chose for a forty-year recap was in a cellar off the Queensway. We filed through a dim, low-ceilinged bar into a dimmer low-ceilinged dining room and sat at at the end of a long wooden table. The place was filled with bright young things who were whooping it up with their yards of beer and the one-man oompah band. One couple, dancing a not-very-expert polka, swung in too close to our table and crashed into it, spilling everybody's drinks and appetizers.

"It's a find, so retro-eighties, you'll love it," Nigel insisted, picking olives out of his lap.

For the first time since I'd met her, I began to like Abby Russell. Here, at this hastily arranged affair, which promised to be awkward and potentially embarrassing, she lifted her chin, pretended she hadn't been pushed in front of a taxi and became positively animated when she explained where she'd been and what she'd been doing for the past four and a half decades. It was an admirable performance, and we all followed her lead, becoming very English and civilized over drinks and dinner, although the noise level was high, and I was only getting every other word. I concentrated on my lamb shank, which was excellent, and the German wine, which was too sweet but went down easily. Nigel made witty remarks at intervals, and Edward listened and watched, blue eyes cautious.

". . . if you remember, I'd planned the trip for several weeks. I hitchhiked to Dover and caught the noon ferry and met some friends in the south of France. And then they were going on to Greece, and I just tagged along."

"France? I thought you were haring off to Coventry that day," Nigel objected. "Funnily enough, though, you never came back. Or wrote, either."

Abby looked away, uncomfortable. "I know. Things were a bit of a mess — you know, with Josef and all that —"

"Ah, yes, Josef. He's divorced yet again. From Reid's mother. Of course, they lived apart for years." When Abby didn't say anything, he shrugged. "So you just left Susan and me holding the rental bag . . ." He frowned as he said the name, and the smile left his face.

"Yes, I know. I'm — I was terribly sorry. I didn't hear about her until much later and by that time I'd met Gerry in Rhodes, and he was going back to the States with some friends, and I, well, he wanted me to go with him. You know how it was in those days, everybody dashing off in all directions with everyone else. And then we got married."

That rendition didn't gel with the notes I had from daughter Sunni, but memory does funny things to us all. Maybe Gerry was so whacked out on crystal blue persuasion he'd forgotten a quick jaunt to Greece. Or maybe Sunni's mother just liked re-editing her past. I continued to listen without comment, except to assure Edward my dinner was excellent when he asked.

"So . . . France, the Greek islands, California, quite a saga. You always did have a mind of your own, darling. And there was Edward," Nigel smirked, "just pining away, awaiting your return."

"Edward?" Abby paused, her eyes confused. "You never married?"

"Twice, actually," Edward said, looking bored.

"Oh." Abby blinked. "I thought . . . Nigel . . ."

Edward shrugged. "Where Nigel is, can spite be far behind?" He ordered another round of drinks before reciting his own brief and ironic resume: fiction writing, abandoned after six years of ego-destroying rejections; one ego-destroying marriage and unpleasant divorce; editing a magazine started by friends; a second ten year marriage also ending in divorce; and finally launching his own art magazine after a stint as freelance photographer for *Rolling Stone* magazine and several newspapers.

Nigel kept missing or ignoring his cue. When Edward finished Abby had another turn, describing her life in California with her husband and daughter. Edward, either transfixed by wine and boredom or honestly mesmerized, was hanging on every word. I caught myself looking for similarities between his face and Sunni Russell's.

At one point Edward asked about me, and I was as terse as he'd been. Born in Ohio, now living in Florida. Former photojournalist based in London for six years, now a part-time college instructor traveling for pleasure. Abby Russell chimed in when she realized I wasn't going to elaborate and painted a glossy picture of me as a talented surfer and patron saint of a houseful of eccentric artists. I drank more wine and allowed it.

It was becoming clear that our reason for being here — in this particular restaurant — was a twentyish kid in lederhosen who trotted out at intervals with a rolling cart to play Alpine bells. Nigel openly ogled him then dropped his eyes and kept repeating the ploy until even Abby got the message. She turned slightly to glance at Edward, and they exchanged a long expressionless look. Edward had known about Nigel, at least, all those years ago.

When the bell ringer rolled back into the kitchen, Nigel sighed out loud and turned to Abby. "Tell me about commune living, darling. Was it really just playing the guitar and dropping acid? Just one glorious non-stop orgy?"

"Not really." Abby's tone was slightly acerbic, and she avoided his gaze. "That was the media. Real communes weren't like that, at least not for long. Charlie Manson may have had sex six times a day, but the rest of us were working. Somebody had to pick crops and cook and do the laundry."

Nigel sighed again, disappointed. "So much for the promised land. Is that why you left, then?"

Abby raised her chin and gazed across the room. "A bit, I suppose. My in-laws wanted us back in the mainstream . . . but . . . I'm embarrassed to say, I think it was the food. I got sick of beans and greens and began to long for steak and shrimp and pork chops." A smile crinkled the corners of her mouth. "And a dress that hadn't been worn by somebody else and a good hair cut and a hot bath every single day. One morning I woke up and my washcloth was frozen to the ground. We left an hour later with a plastic bag of belongings and bus fare home. We looked like Okies fleeing the Dust Bowl, only we still had our teeth."

Nigel's eyes widened. "You gave up peace and love and the utopian dream for a little extra grub and some creature comforts?"

She lifted an elegant shoulder and let it drop. "The communes were failing by then, completely out of control. People kept turning up for the free food so they could save their welfare checks for drugs. Not much peace and love to spare, just heroin and disillusionment and brain dead junkies." She gave Nigel a level, ironic look. "Remember the American comic strip Pogo, 'We have met the enemy, and he is us'? Well, the common enemy was no longer the establishment."

"That's an amazingly objective view," Edward said. "How did you manage to grasp what was actually happening in the very midst of it all?"

"I didn't." Abby turned the ironic look in his direction. "I grasped it fifteen years later. Two credit hours at University of Southern California: The Utopian Commune and the Counter Culture."

The evening, cobbled together by old memories and good manners, began to deteriorate when Nigel drained the rest of his beer, leaned forward into one of the candles on the table and caught his hair on fire. Edward daubed out the fire to the cheers of the other patrons, who were going to let him burn, and suggested we leave. Nigel refused and ordered a round of something called ApfelKorn, which arrived in colored shot glasses on an iced tray.

"Don't touch the stuff," Edward advised me, "it doesn't freeze." He threw a handful of twenty pound notes on the table and went to find a taxi.

"Let's get together while you're in town, darling." Nigel fumbled a card out of his pocket as Abby and I got to our feet. "Ring me tomorrow. The old Abby never ducked out of the party early, and I still have a slew of questions. Like what about the money? Did you really just go away leaving your investment without asking for any of it back? Or did Josef give you traveling cash and not tell anyone?"

Abby pocketed his card without answering and headed for the stairs to the street, as if wolves were nipping at her heels. The air outside was damp and cold, more like April than June, but it was a relief after the crowded basement.

As we rolled down Bayswater Road, the silence inside the taxi was as substantial as a fourth, less friendly passenger. Abby Russell's face was grim in the lights from the street; I thought she had tears in her eyes.

Edward shifted uncomfortably in the jump seat and began talking in a determined voice about London, circa 1966. "Remember how we used to pool our shillings and hire a cab to take us along the Embankment at three in the morning?" he reminisced. "When we heard Big Ben strike, we'd get the morning papers as they rolled right off the presses and cab back to the flat for fried eggs and chips."

"When we had eggs. Or potatoes." Abby made an effort, but her voice was almost a whisper. "What's happened to him? To Nigel? He was never like that. So acidic."

Instead of answering, Edward leaned sideways and spoke to the driver, "Take us down along the Embankment."

The driver, a Pakistani, was obviously delighted to be with us. He raced down Pall Mall, as if it were a drag strip and swung us around the south end of Trafalgar Square with expertise. Only one person lolled in the mouth of a huge black lion tonight, and the tourists were all wearing coats.

"Remember when you threw your shoes out the taxi window here?" Edward said to Abby.

She seemed to come back from a far distant place. "Not me, I'm afraid. That was Susan."

Edward thought for a second. "Correct. They were your shoes, though. Black pumps. You'd lent them to her, and you were quite cross about it. Susan didn't drink as a rule," he explained to me, "but that night she was definitely one over the eight. Giggling hysterical, totally out of control. Nearly beaned a kid on a cycle."

The cab slowed as we reached the river and progressed along a night-time Thames edged in glittering lights and ancient magic.

"Millennium Bridge," the driver announced in a thick accent.

I looked out, prepared to dislike it on principle. Instead, whoever dubbed it the blade-of-light had gotten it right. It was graceful, sharp-edged and gleaming against the dark purple sky.

Edward continued to chatter. ". . . might have been poor and starving, but we always had salt and pepper and plenty of tea. We'd snatch a bottle of milk off the neighbor's doorstep now and again when we got sick of drinking it black. And one lovely day the butcher delivered a packet of pork chops to the front door by mistake. Nigel fried them up, and we wolfed them down before the delivery boy realized his error. I can still remember the taste. A world away from the cream cakes and milky tea we lived on at the gallery. Liz," he turned to me, "that's Josef's first wife, was generally good for a handout, but when Susan came along things got much better. She cooked up all sorts of concoctions."

By the time we pulled up in front of the Abbott Hotel it was raining again. Even so, Edward escorted us through the cold mist to the front entrance and said he'd call the following day, before hustling back to the cab. Abby, looking significantly more cheerful, was smiling after him when she realized I had de-cabbed with her.

"I — I'm so sorry, we've let the taxi go. Where are you staying?"

"I'm at the Saxon," I waved a hand up the street, "but it's only twelve o'clock. Does your hotel have a bar? We need to talk."

She hesitated for a few seconds, then nodded. "I guess."

Chapter 8

Neither of us wanted another drink. Abby charmed the night man into bringing us tea instead, and we sat in the deserted lobby.

I settled back in a pile of squishy leather and eyed her. Now that we were sitting here alone, ready for a heart-to-heart, I was sorry I'd suggested it. How do you ask somebody you don't really know what the hell's going on? I searched for tactful words, didn't like the ones I found, and shifted uncomfortably in my chair. Finally I said, surprising both of us, "Did somebody really push you in front of that cab?"

Abby Russell's green eyes widened and her mouth opened for at least five seconds before any words came out. "I thought so. Fingers jabbed into my back. But it must have been an accident. I mean, there's no reason . . ."

"Was Edward where you could see him all the time?"

"Edward? No, he was getting the cab."

"You saw him get it?"

"Well, no, he went out in the street while I waited, but —"

"And you didn't see Nigel or Josef or Josef's girlfriend? Standing around outside?"

"No, of course, not." She frowned as if I were crazy. "They didn't push me. Is that what you're saying?"

"How do you know?"

"I . . . I just know. And anyway, Steven said —"

"Oh, right, Steven. Did Steven mention anybody else who might want to give you a little shove?"

"Of course not." A wary look replaced the frown on her face. "He just said I'd have to be careful. But he said help was on the way."

"Help? Psychic help? Like the kind you'd meet on the plane coming over?"

"Well," she paused, "he did say somebody with a feel for the past. Carlo was the one who talked about a psychic. He said to look for the initials S and K. Steven just said K." She moved her purse from her lap to the floor and leaned forward. "I couldn't believe my luck when you told me your name, but I hate flying, and I'd had a lot to drink. When I woke up I felt awful, and all I could remember was babbling on about my personal business. I was embarrassed, and I just wanted to — to get away and forget all about it. And then I thought I'd really messed it up. Still, when I talked to Steven long distance, he said you'd turn up again if it was the right thing. That's why I was so relieved when I saw you at the gallery tonight."

"Okay." I had already decided what to do. I gave it a three count and said, "I am supposed to look out for you while you're here. But in spite of Carlos and the initials, I'm not any kind of psychic."

At that moment the tea arrived on a small tray. Mrs. Russell frowned at it but didn't move. I picked up the pot, poured a cup and slid it in her direction. I poured a second cup for me and drank half of it before continuing. "Didn't you think it was a huge coincidence when I turned up at the gallery tonight? Didn't you wonder what I was doing there?"

She stared at me across the low table. "I thought I knew. Who are you then? And why are you supposed to look after me?"

"Your daughter."

"Oh." It was a very small sound. The expression on her face slipped from wary to hunted.

"She found out you were making this trip secretly. She thinks you've come to meet her real father."

"Oh, damn. I haven't. That's not — no."

"So what is it you're doing? If you haven't had any contact with these people in forty-some years, how'd you know where to find them?"

For a second I didn't think she was going to answer, and neither did she. Then she picked up her cup and let out a long sighing breath. "Detectives, of course. It wasn't hard to find Josef, he still owns the gallery. And Nigel still lurks about. I always thought he looked up to Josef, like a younger brother or something, but I — I may have had it wrong. Nigel's an art consultant now, a bit of a high flyer, they tell me. Edward wasn't hard to track down, either. His magazine does surprisingly well, and he covers a lot of gallery first nights. Steven," she flashed a defiant look at me, "said they'd all be here together in June, so I arranged to fly over."

"But if you knew they'd be there, why did you faint when you saw Josef and the girl?"

"I —" she paused and sipped at her tea "I didn't realize he'd look so much older, I guess. And jet lag and drinking too much and not eating. I just ran out of steam."

"You looked a little shaky when you saw the headless paintings too."

"Well, I was. They bothered me quite a lot. Susan did some like that years ago. It was upsetting to see them."

I wasn't entirely convinced, but I let it go. "Why bother paying detectives when you had all that psychic input?"

Her frown came back. "I wanted to be absolutely sure. But Steven said they were tied together intrinsically, and he was right. He's always right. Josef, Nigel, Edward — all exactly when he said they'd be. Not Liz, though, Josef's first wife. They divorced long ago. Steven's always right on the money," she added, sounding defensive, "and why I ever went to Carlo I'll never know. I suppose this is all complete gibberish to you."

She straightened and seemed to take a grip on herself. "I've come back to . . . bury my dead. I'd like to live the next twenty years freer than I've lived the last forty-seven. But I'm going to need help, I can see that, which is why I'm talking to you now about my very personal, private business." She lifted her chin and the green eyes grew more determined. "Steven said I could trust you like, well, like family. He said you'd be reluctant, but you'd do the right thing," She slid back in her chair. "Look, I'm not the wuss I must seem. I'm a reasonably intelligent woman — one lucky enough to find a man who loved and provided for her, but after I decided to come here," she looked away, "I'm that gutless girl again. The one who ran away. I want the woman back. The self I worked so hard for all those years."

"Hold on." I refused to be deterred by psycho-hooey. "Where did you go by taxi at nine-thirty this morning?"

"This morning?"

I had her attention. I waited.

"Oh, Selfridges. To get my hair done. Why?"

"And yesterday?"

"Yesterday? To Earls Court where we used to live. I wanted to see the flat again. And then to the gallery." For a moment she seemed bemused. "Do you know, I trekked clear across town on the Underground before I even thought of a taxi? As Edward said, taxis were pretty much a treat in the old days. That twenty-year-old girl again." She paused for a moment. "Why are you asking? Have you been following me around?"

"Yes, as instructed." I had a sudden, very weird thought. "Do you have a long, blonde wig?"

She made a face. "Why would I have something like that?"

"You don't have one?"

"Of course not, nobody wears wigs any more — unless they're sick. Listen, Steven said the answer was here. With the people here, but I realize . . . I need a plan. Did you ever do any rebirthings?"

The shift in subject threw me. "Excuse me?"

"Rebirthings, like hypnosis, life regressions." Her eyes slid away, and she twisted her fingers together. "You see, I forgot — actually forgot — about Susan once I was in California. It's like having a snake in your house. At first you're scared to death all the time, and then you forget every once in a while, and after several years, it just goes out of your mind and stays out." She glanced up to see if I was still with her. "But the snake is always there, really. After Gerry died I started having horrible dreams. That's how I ended up with Steven. We did these rebirthings, and he told me to face my demons . . . in person. He said we always exit through the same door we came in. The answer's here, waiting. I just need some help figuring it out."

I sat looking at her, trying to integrate the perfect hair, sophisticated clothes and normal appearance with the New Age conversation. She, at least, knew what she was talking about.

"On the plane you said you knew who killed Susan Miachi,

who it had to be," I reminded her.

"Did I? Well, I don't. I don't know anybody who could do something so absolutely dreadful."

"Then why spend years hiding out in California."

"That's not . . . Are you being paid?"

"Excuse me?"

"How much is Sunni paying you to look after me?"

"Oh. Airfare and expenses."

"So what you said on the plane wasn't so, either. You're really a detective."

"No, I told you the truth. I met your daughter through a friend. I refused to do what she wanted initially. But she got the friend to convince me. Sunni's worried about you. She thinks you have cancer."

"The friend was a man, I suppose. With Sunni, it's always a man; that's how she gets things done." Her head snapped up. "Cancer? I don't have cancer."

"No?"

"Absolutely not. I just want to know what happened all those years ago. Make sure it wasn't my fault."

"You were in France. How could it be your fault?"

"And I expect you'd better help me." She went on as if she hadn't heard. "After all, you are being paid, you know more about me than practically anyone else at this point, and, besides, you're a writer — a journalist."

"Not anymore." I frowned. "Anyway, photojournalists don't write, just try to spell correctly and get the right caption on the right picture."

"But you have credentials. People will talk to anybody with credentials. I'll write the questions, and you can say you're researching a story about Susan's life, I mean death. It'll be the truth. I'll pay you to write it myself."

"Your daughter's already paying me. She'll probably be furious when she finds out I told you about it."

"That's easy then, don't tell her. I never do."

I grinned at her. "Not exactly ethical . . ."

"If you're not a detective, you've got no code of ethics. And we wouldn't be paying you for the same thing at all."

"What would I say when I reported in to your daughter?"

"Tell her I've hired you to help me investigate my past."

"With the understanding that I continue to report where you go and who you see?"

She stared at me for a second. "That shouldn't hurt anything. Just tell her I'm trying to find out what happened to an old friend."

"She may misunderstand. Sunni's looking for her father . . ."

Whatever energy she'd been running on oozed away right in front of me.

"I know she is," she admitted. "We'll just have to — we'll cross that rickety old bridge when we come to it." She picked up her purse from the floor and got to her feet as if everything was settled.

I stayed put in my chair. "I'm not sure this is a good idea," I told her, "but if I agree to do it, I need information. All I know is that you and Nigel and Susan shared a basement flat in Earls Court in 1966, that Edward lived in the same building, and that you invested some money in Josef's gallery."

She sank down slowly in the chair she was trying to vacate. "I don't think that's the best way — to proceed. What if I'm wrong? You should just talk to them first . . . and then I'll say whether it was that way or not."

I thought about it, then said, "Uh, uh. You don't have to be right about anything. Just tell me what you remember about Susan."

An expression of distaste crossed her face. "I hate rehashing the past."

"You must be used to it after all that re-birthing. Start with the good stuff first. What's your strongest memory of London in 1966."

"The strongest? Well, strongest certainly isn't best. Mostly I remember how dreadfully cold it was in the flat. By November we had frost inside the windows mornings. There was a two bar heater, but one bar didn't work, and we had to move it from room to room. The bathroom was always like ice, tub water cold by the time you finished running it."

"Good." I grinned at her in encouragement. "And outside?"

"Deadly. I used to pray for rain. It had to warm up to rain." Her mouth twisted in a half smile. "Even indoors we went 'round in wooly scarves and gloves and caps. We were always buying chestnuts — the hot roasted sort from the street vendors. Thruppence for a little shiny brown paper bag, and if you put a bag in each coat pocket, your hands stayed warm for maybe eight minutes. The Underground was freezing, wind blowing down the tunnels and paper scraps and grit flying up in all directions."

She slid back in her chair and hugged her arms around her body, as if remembering the cold too well. "The only warm places were the clubs; the best one was in a Soho basement. It wasn't glamorous. You walked through narrow little streets lined with empty produce crates and grubby dust bins. The scent of rotting oranges permeated everything. But when you opened the club door, the smell of pot and sweat and stale beer was even stronger. Inside, it was like nothing I'd ever seen — huge, dark room, colored lights flashing, micro-minis, gyrating bodies. Most of the women were braless; some were dancing topless. There was always a band playing on a platform at the back of the room. You could hardly see them for the cigarette smoke."

Abby Russell was smiling to herself as she remembered. "Mick Jagger used to hang out there talking to the band all night because nobody bothered him for autographs. And there were always Americans around. A girl named Mary used to sit around on one of the couches stark naked. I could never figure out how she got there in nothing at all — no coat, no shoes. She was always sharing grass that looked like rough brown tea and telling us how great this commune in San Francisco was and how they'd take in anybody."

Abby leaned forward across the table, her face animated. "It sounds naïve now, doesn't it? But the clubs were happening places back then. None of that chilly English reserve or disapproval; strangers actually spoke to each other, and you could do what you wanted . . . no guilt . . ." She drew in a sharp breath, frowned, and then continued with less enthusiasm. "There really was going to be a brave new world, and we were all going to be part of it. It wasn't just about drugs like it was later."

She kept the frown as she settled back in her chair. Something had stopped the easy flow of reminiscence, some memory that was apparently going to remain private.

"So, what about Susan?" I said. "Did she like the club scene too?"

"Well, Susan was more uptight than everybody else, I guess. She'd met her ex-husband at a club, and it left a bad taste in her mouth. She wasn't into drugs, and she didn't like weekend hippies."

"Weekend what?"

"You know, drunks or married men who came hoping free love was a literal term."

"What about Josef and Edward?"

She raised a shoulder and let it fall with a sigh of resignation. "Edward was trying to finish his book and never had time, and

Josef — well, Josef had better things to do than hang around blissed-out hippies who spent the evening making friends with the furniture. He actually said that once. Josef only liked 'real art' and everybody else was into psychedelic light shows and the Beatles and Radio Caroline — you know, the pirate station that played pop music all day long. Josef was older than the rest of us, ten years or so, and more controlled."

"Not the type to run off to the commune with naked Mary?"

"No, but life's a surprise, isn't it? Eventually, I ended up in one myself." She raised her chin and narrowed those green eyes at me. "Is that enough information for now? Enough probing into my checkered past?"

I looked at my watch, saw it was well after midnight, and grinned at her. "Enough to get started. You'll set up the interviews?"

She nodded as she got to her feet. "All you have to do is show up and take notes."

Sounded easy to me.

Chapter 9

Mrs. Russell was either more organized or more motivated than I'd expected.

In one day she signed up Nigel and Edward, neither of whom objected to discussing Susan Miachi, and got the girl at the gallery to pencil us into Josef's schedule. She wasn't able to reach Josef's ex-wife, Liz, but said she thought Edward could help since he still kept in touch with her.

I did my part, shopping Oxford Street for a miniature tape recorder, brushing up on my reporter impersonations, and calling daughter Sunni to report my conversation with her mother. Again Sunni surprised me by not being upset. For a redhead, she was amazingly laid back. In fact, she insisted on giving me credit I didn't deserve, even when I explained it was all Abby Russell's idea.

"Very smart," she enthused. "I knew you'd figure out a way to do it. I'm working on Worth Avenue right now, but you call the second you know anything. Oh, and Tom said if I talked to you to say hello and he'll be in touch soon."

Really?

I scowled at the phone as I snapped it shut. First he couldn't wait to get rid of me, and now he was sending messages through painter girl? I nearly dialed him on the spot but held back as a little badly needed self-respect kicked in. If he was so hot and heavy with Sunni that he couldn't punch in my number, did I want to know about it? Worrying about Tom Roddler could keep 'til later; it always did. Better to concentrate on what I was being paid to do — help Abby Russell figure out what happened to her friend Susan.

Exactly thirty-seven hours after our Tiroler Hut dinner, Abby and I took a cab to St. Paul's Cathedral and crossed the Millennium Bridge to the Tate Modern Art Museum. The bridge wasn't as spectacular in daylight as it was at night; in fact, it was just a gray, nondescript walkway. Since we were early for a lunch date with Nigel, who'd picked the restaurant, we took our time, stopping halfway across to look up and down the river.

The sun was out, and the Thames was a spectacular blue, a blue that almost matched the sky. Then a fast moving bank of angry clouds began rolling in from the west. By the time we reached the Tate, both sky and river were dark gray. I hoped it wasn't some weird kind of omen.

Abby had managed to avoid any additional Sixties reminiscing, and the interview questions she promised never materialized. Her plan of attack, however, wasn't complicated.

She and I would meet with each of the people who were directly involved with Susan Miachi in 1966: Josef, Edward, Nigel and hopefully, Liz, Josef's ex. During the conversation, Abby would be called away or have an emergency appointment, and I would continue to ask whatever questions occurred to me. She was convinced they would say things in her absence they would never say in her presence.

She was not wrong.

"Abby was always a jumped up little bitch, really," Nigel remarked as he watched her walk out of the Tate's seventh floor restaurant. "Still, marrying money is obviously mellowing. And it was nice of her to get the check. Haddock and chips are a bit dear here," he peered into his glass of red wine. "and this is definitely not plonk. Seats are hard, though."

Nigel seemed less stagey than he had been at the Tiroler Hut; he'd left his red leisure suit home. Except that his hair was shorter where he'd trimmed the singed pieces, there was little evidence of our boozy night out. He had behaved himself at lunch, chatted nicely and asked no embarrassing questions about Josef or borrowed money.

"Abby came straight off a farm in Lancashire, you know." He set his glass down and grinned at me. "Her parents were free Presbyterian or some off brand, and they saved every tuppence. When they died she got the lot. Came up to town with her pockets full of pounds and attached herself like a limpet to Josef, who turned her nondescript brown hair to glowing russet, melted four stone off her one way and another, and made her a receptionist at the Edgware Road Gallery." He made a face. "They call them *galleristas* now. Anyway, the farm money found its way out of her pocket into his and, voilà! Josef's at Jubilee Walk emerged from the ashes of a less up-market address."

He lit a cigarette and eyed me over a stream of smoke. "He also landed her on me as a roommate in my nice Earls Court flat. Does she really have an unbreakable appointment or is she just leaving so I'll talk about Susan with an unbridled tongue?"

"She really has an appointment," I lied. "Are you allowed to smoke in here?"

"Not really." He put out the pale green cigarette on the sole of his shoe, dropped the stub in his pocket and looked innocent as a waiter headed our way, hesitated and stood watching uncertainly. "Only those few forbidden puffs before they cast you into outer darkness, but, oh, what glorious puffs they are."

I smiled at him. I couldn't help it. "Are you going to?"

"Going to what? Tell you about Susan? Certainly." He sighed. "Actually, I don't like talking about her. There's nothing bad to say, and that's too boring for words."

When I didn't respond he eventually turned sideways, draped one cream colored pant leg over the other and settled more comfortably in his chair.

"Susan turned up on our doorstep one coolish day in September. Huge surprise to me, but Abby thought her rent was too high, and we could squeeze one more person into *my* basement flat." He raised an eyebrow. "Remember those old third girl adverts? No, of course you wouldn't. Well, it was the done thing in those days, and I did have three twin beds in *the* bedroom. No closet space at all, just a smallish wardrobe barely large enough for me. I was livid, but there was this sweet faced American girl in a Dartmouth sweatshirt with one long braid down her back, nineteen years old but looking twelve, saying she'd seen the ad and had we filled the spot yet." He looked out the windows at the Thames below. "Girls cohabiting with boys was quite new in those days; you could see she thought she was doing something daring." He sighed. "Susan was nice to everybody. After a bit, she even rubbed off on Abby, who became quite a lot more human for a time."

"Abby said Susan painted."

He nodded. "Night and day. Set up her easel in front of the French doors to get what light there was." He reached for his cigarettes, remembered, and buried his hands in his pockets. "She'd be there when I came home, daubed with paint, arms waving, hair a mess, panting like a person possessed . . ."

"Really?"

"Some do it that way. I don't think she ever had a lesson, just a lot of passion. I took her to see Josef; he let her work at the gallery when she wanted and hang a few of her small canvasses. A couple of them sold."

"Were they headless? Mrs. Russell said Beijing's headless pictures were like ones Susan had done."

"Well," he frowned at me, "some were, but Susan's paintings were disturbing. Beijing's are — dare I say? — shallowish. I expect Josef gave her the idea in a moment of weakness. God knows she needs ideas."

"Did Josef give Susan a makeover too? Like Abby?"

"No." He looked startled. "Susan was a knockout. True, Josef had a thing for redheads but he kept off Susan. Abby would have killed him for one thing, and Susan lacked the requisite wild streak. She was probably the only person in London who didn't have sex in 1966, so it was a shock when the papers said the dead girl was several months along." He shrugged. "Particularly Edward, who didn't realize he'd been chasing someone with a bun in the oven. And particularly since he'd just shifted his affections to her from Abby under somewhat similar circumstances. But you'll have had all that from Abby. Anything else in particular, love? Because I should probably get moving."

"Just a couple of things. Did you have to identify Susan? When they found her?"

"No, that was Edward. They called him downstairs to — to

look. I was in Mallorca with friends, thank God, and didn't know until the following week. The flat was a disaster, of course. Edward and I both moved out and so did the people above him."

I made a couple of notes. "Thanks. I guess that's . . . unless you could just give me a quick impression of the people associated with the gallery?"

"A one-off of each?" His eyes glittered. "I think I could manage that. Who first?"

"Edward?"

Nigel raised an eyebrow. "Frustrated novelist but multitalented. The worst kind. Placates himself by writing nasty things about rising new artists. Had a fling with Abby when she first moved in; it cooled when he discovered he was sharing with Josef and various others. Does considerable charity work these days — for his sins. Still sees Liz, Josef's first ex wife, who definitely falls in that category. Sorry for her, I think."

"Really. Where is she now? Liz?"

He shrugged. "I haven't asked. She's somewhere, I suppose, and wherever she is, she's pissed."

"In the English sense as in drunk? Or American as in irritated?"

"Oh, the second, dear one. I tend to be multilingual." He hesitated. "Liz was a bright, attractive blonde in the Sixties. Now she has an iffy face lift, thinning hair and weighs fifteen stone. That's 195 pounds to you, darling. She's also the PDQ." He laughed at the blank look on my face. "Prescription Drug Queen. Never remarried, of course. Never found anyone who craved a daily dose of bitterness."

"How about Beijing?"

He made a face and shrugged. "As the Tuscans say, 'Icche c'e c'e'. *What you see is what you get*."

"And that's it?"

"No. To be absolutely fair, there's probably more, but it's all been stuffed and molded into Josef's dream girl. All that escapes the mold is an increasingly bad temper and a gift for creating art with great enthusiasm and little technique."

"What about Reid?" I had meant to say Joseph, but Reid's name tumbled right off my tongue instead.

Nigel eyed me for a thoughtful moment. "The boy wonder? The man who would be king? Let's see — self-involved, hates his father's latest protégée, smarter than he looks, and quite, quite dishy." He raised an eyebrow. "If the boy wants you and he has time to spend on it, you might just as well do as the Victorian newlyweds: lean back, close your eyes and think of England."

I didn't ask if he was speaking from experience. "And his father? Josef?"

"Self-involved, hates his latest protégée . . ."

I raised an eyebrow in a parody of his.

He smiled. "He hates them all in the end, does Josef. Brings them along, makes them look like . . . well, alike. Tires when the dream wears thin."

"Look like who?"

"Our Abby, I've always thought. He never got over her . . . for whatever reason." He smiled again. "Josef has quite a paper trail — ex-wives, girlfriends, babies. He clings to it as he clings to the Chelsea of his youth, even though the art world is all East Side nowadays. In the end, though, he's still an upstart from Hungary who got out ahead of the Russian tanks with a change of underwear and five bob."

"Josef's Hungarian?"

He grinned, reached across and pinched my cheek. "Last time he looked, Americano."

We walked out to the elevators together. Nigel pushed the down button and said, "Abby failed to mention at dinner that her little surfer friend was also a journalist. Freelance or legitimate press for this project?"

I shrugged and smiled at him.

"Not talking?" He pointed a finger down the hall. "See those big Plexiglas tubes? If you sign a release and don elbow pads, they'll put you on a little canvas toboggan and zip your hapless body to the ground floor like a message in a pneumatic tube. *'The very latest in participation art from Unilever.'* "

"Really?" I thought about it. "I might."

He nodded. "You look the adventurous type. But don't forget to wander about first. The Tate Modern has everything. Picasso, Matisse, Andy Warhol. Even Steve McQueen, believe it or not. Then come to the East End, and I'll show you art that'll knock your starched socks off."

I waved goodbye but decided against the tour. I'd had enough culture for a while, and I wanted to get some of Nigel's comments down on paper before I forgot them.

The canvas sleds were just as Nigel promised. I went from the seventh floor to the floor of Turbine Hall in twenty adrenaline-filled seconds.

Chapter 10

An overcrowded tube train isn't the greatest place for making notes, but I stuck with it all the way to Bloomsbury.

I could have saved myself the trouble by using my tiny new recorder, but I'd decided against it. People speak differently when they know they're being taped, and I hadn't wanted to sneak on Nigel. For once, that was probably the right decision. Just from the information he'd shared, I was pretty sure I could name Sunni Russell's father.

I was beginning to like this private journalism gig. Instead of taking hundreds of pictures (and hoping for two good ones), nursing sore feet and living on chips, I got salary, haute cuisine and traveling money. It wasn't much like work, and I was looking forward to eating my way through our second interview this evening, one with Edward, at a place called The Little Prince in Camden Lock.

In the meantime, while Abby Russell occupied herself with a little retail therapy at Liberty, I finished the notes, dropped them by my hotel, and took a taxi to Westminster Abbey. There, with a few hundred other tourists, I spent the afternoon looking at the tombs of assorted Royals, poets, statesmen and writers. They had a better philosophy concerning death in the old days: much better to be bronzed and borne on a bier by six or seven gorgeous male statues than reduced to ashes and scattered over the natural resource of your choice.

By dinner time I was on my way to Camden Lock in northeast London. I took the tube all the way there just to prove I could.

Edward, with Abby Russell in tow, arrived by water bus from Little Venice. They'd been out seeing the sights, she said. Her hair was wind-tossed, she was smiling nonstop and she looked about thirty. She'd either ditched the jet lag completely or Edward was titillating company. So to speak.

Camden Town was a little more high tech than I remembered, but it still had a working lock, red and yellow and green canal boats, and outdoor markets. You could buy everything from Moroccan saddle chairs to joss sticks there; people from all over the world mingled happily with the updated version of punks and Goths.

The Little Prince was an anomaly in Camden Lock — no tongue studs, no cutting edge music, no wireless hookups. It was barely big enough for its seven tables and the seventh was squashed against the front door. If you liked candle light, rough pine tables and a cold breeze gusting in every time the door opened to new patrons, it was paradise.

Abby Russell ate her share of some outstanding chicken cous cous, picked up the check over Edward's objections, and departed, ostensibly to take a business call at her hotel. That left Edward and me with cardamom tea and the subject of Susan Miachi.

Edward was absolutely my kind of guy. Too old, technically, but age is relative when balanced by thick silver hair, a lean body and great charm. Robert Redford with fewer wrinkles, I mused, forcing my attention back to the conversation.

". . . they asked me to go downstairs and identify her," he was saying. "Horrible. Face all bashed about, clothes charred, sweatshirt partially burned away, God-awful smell. Hell of a way to get your fifteen minutes of fame."

"You didn't hear anything that afternoon? Even though you were writing in the flat?"

He shook his head. "I wouldn't have, not unless the windows were wide open or they were having a party. I didn't even know there was a fire until the police came 'round."

"You didn't smell smoke?"

"No, but when I'm working I tune out. It wasn't much of a fire, really, but someone must have noticed and rung the police from a call box outside Earls Court station. It was in the papers for weeks. All the Aussies and Canadians in the area were locking their doors and staying in at night. Then it came out that Susan was pregnant and had run away from her husband. He was Mafia apparently — one of those American things. It did explain a lot."

"Like what?"

"Well, why she kept such a low profile, refused to sign her paintings, that sort of thing. She'd only initial them, and Josef was always on at her about it. He was devastated when she was killed, didn't show up at the gallery for days. And when Abby left too, without a word, well, it . . . everything changed."

"But for you especially?"

He stared at me across the table. "I'm not certain what you mean."

"Nigel said . . ."

"Oh, well, Nigel's a bit twisted, you know."

"So you weren't interested in her? Susan?"

A smile curved the corners of his mouth. "Of course I was interested. I was twenty-two years old, a long way from Toronto and on the path to greatness. I was interested in everyone and everything." He paused. "You got fonder of Susan the longer you were around her. She was very beautiful, and she had a — kindness — that was a definite turn on." He reached in his pocket and pulled out a thick envelope, which he slid across the table to me. "I brought these. They show it better than I could tell it. Mind you, nobody had a decent camera back then. She's the one in the pink raincoat."

I pulled out a bundle of three-inch-by-three-inch faded color prints and got my first look at Susan Miachi. She was standing in front of Big Ben with two young guys and another girl. The boys had thick caps of hair grazing the tops of their eyebrows and the girls had red hair falling past their shoulders and wispy bangs. All four of them had smooth, baby faces. I glanced up at Edward.

"I can hardly tell which is you and which is Nigel."

"I expect not. We were practically in uniform, John Lennon haircuts, jackets, jeans." He laughed. "And the girls were both going for The Shrimp look. You know, Jean Shrimpton, the world's first super model? She was more blonde, really, but every girl in London wanted that long, tumbling hair."

"I thought Twiggy was the Sixties thing."

He shrugged. "Depended whether you liked waif-like or glamorous."

I held the picture next to the candle for more light. "Abby looks more sophisticated, older than Susan."

"Actually Susan was older, by six months or so. We celebrated Abby's birthday a week before . . . it happened." He picked up the photograph and stared at it. He shook his head. "Funny, the rest of us wouldn't have been caught dead in front of Big Ben in those days. Totally uncool. But Susan loved all the tourist things."

I flipped through the other pictures: Susan and Abby at St. Paul's Cathedral, the Houses of Parliament and Carnaby Street, all four of them at the maze at Hampton Court. Even in his pre-professional years, Edward had an instinct for good light and composition. I placed the remaining photos on the table.

He touched the next to last photo, one of the two girls and Nigel in front of a seedy looking basement door in a seedy looking part of town. "This was taken outside one of the clubs. Nigel and Abby were the night people, really; the rest of us preferred Dim Sum in Soho's Chinese restaurants on Sunday morning — beef dumplings, turnip cake. And afterwards we'd take a bus to one of the hotels near the British Museum and have coffee in the lobby, read the Sunday Times, then go see the current museum exhibit — Korean kimonos or whatnot. We always finished with the mummy rooms. Susan loved the mummy rooms."

The last one was a picture of Nigel and the two girls standing with Josef in front of the Gallery at Jubilee Walk.

I looked at Edward. "Any chance Josef might have been the father of Susan's baby?"

His head was shaking before I got it out. "She wasn't that kind of girl." He gathered up the photos, stacking them carefully. "I know how cliché it sounds, but Susan was more the cosseting type. The one who insisted Nigel and Abby and I eat at least one vegetable a day. Before Susan, we lived on whatever we carted away in our pockets from posh cocktail parties. On freezing cold days she'd run up to my flat and say she'd made a pot of Texas chili something or other and light candles and tell us stories about her job while we ate it." He peered down at his interlaced fingers, as if memories rested there.

"Susan worked part time at a free birth control clinic, and there was always some new drama. Indian women coming in and delivering twins on the floor. Hippies dropping their pants to be checked for venereal diseases. She used to say the clinic's clientele were uniformly un-embar-assed. We thought that quite funny." He shook his head. "She wouldn't have wasted time on Josef. And he was too much taken up with Abby anyway. They — well, she'll have told you."

I shook my head. "She hasn't said anything at all about their relationship."

"Interesting," he murmured. "Abby was always willing to discuss everything: your transgressions, her transgressions, the bus conductor's . . ."

I shrugged. "People change. Sometimes they get a shock and it alters their whole life."

"Do they?" He continued to look at his hands, engrossed in his own thoughts.

After a long, quiet minute, I recapped. "Okay, so Nigel was in Spain when Susan died, you were writing in your flat and Abby was hitchhiking to France, right?"

Edward shrugged. "That's what she said, but it wasn't her style. Most likely she was meeting Josef at some hotel for a bit of slap and tickle."

"Abby didn't hitchhike?"

"Well, she did, if necessary; but she was impatient and reckless. She and Susan and I went to Shrewsbury once, and Abby took rides with anybody: Cypriot freedom fighters, old men coming out of pubs too blind to drive. Once she got us a lift with a bloke who was likely a contract killer. We could see the gun sticking out of his shoulder holster, but only after we got in the car." He laughed softly. "After that, Susan would only travel by train. Which was why I wasn't surprised to find out she hadn't gone to Stratford that day."

"Wait a minute. Was Susan supposed to be away too? The day she died?"

"As I remember. Abby went off early on the Saturday — to Coventry, she said — and Nigel was in Spain, Mallorca, actually. Susan left around nine or ten. She wanted to see a play, Shakespeare, the Avon, all that, but the train only went to the nearest town. You had to get a cab or wait for an inconvenient bus." He shrugged. "Susan didn't waste money on cabs. It was one of her things, although she spent any amount on paint and canvas and feeding us." He let out a long, deep breath. "I wanted to finish a couple of chapters, and I said if she'd wait until Sunday, I'd go too. She didn't want to wait."

"Except she didn't go?"

"She must have come back for some reason. They found her about three o'clock Saturday afternoon. Down there in the flat all the time, and I didn't even know." His frown got deeper, and the blue eyes went almost gray.

"What you said, about people getting a shock and changing. What sort of shock? You don't think Abby . . ."

"Why not? What if she wasn't off backpacking or meeting Josef? What if she came back to the flat and found Susan dead and phoned the police from the call box outside the Underground station?"

Edward looked appalled. "And just ran away and never came back? Why would she do something like that?"

"You might, if you were young and scared to death. Or suppose she actually saw someone she recognized. In the flat or in the street close by. And suppose she didn't want to believe that person had anything to do with it or get him in trouble. So she ran away to California and stayed there."

Edward's eyes narrowed to slits. "That's a lot of supposing. Abby was very close to Susan. There's no way she'd let someone hurt her. Unless . . ."

"Unless it had already happened, and she was more attached to the person who did it than she was to Susan?"

Edward pushed his tea cup to one side of the table and leaned back on the wooden bench. "What sort of article is it you're writing? I hope you won't suggest that one of Susan's friends had anything to do with her death. I was the only one even in town at the time. Josef was on a buying trip somewhere, and Liz, his then wife, had gone to relatives in Surrey or Kent. It was quite understood at the time that it was the ex-husband."

"If so, wouldn't the police have caught him almost immediately? He'd have to show a passport to get out of the country."

"Perhaps he hired someone or had a fake passport. Not a problem for the Mafia."

"Maybe so." I leaned toward him and let it go. "Before I forget, I understand you're still friends with Liz — Josef's ex."

"I wouldn't say friends, exactly. We chat now and again."

"I was wondering if you could arrange for us to talk to her."

He gave me a dubious look. "I don't know that she would. It was such a long time ago. I doubt she'd want to see Abby again — or relive those days."

"She's found a kind of peace and doesn't want to be disturbed?"

"I wouldn't say that."

"You could be there too, if it would help. I'm really doing this for Abby, as you know, and it would have to be soon. We're only here a couple of weeks."

Edward shook his head. "The best I could do would be a phone call."

"I'd appreciate it." I picked up the pictures. "Could I keep these for a few days?"

"Of course, I'd just like them back when you've finished."

I slipped the photos back in their envelope and dropped it in my bag. "About Nigel and Josef, what was the relationship there?"

"Difficult to say. There was a lot of experimenting back then. Nigel was actually closer to Liz at first, but he idolized Josef. He was furious when Abby undercut him by getting pregnant. After all, we'd had the pill in the UK for six years."

"Abby was pregnant too? And Josef was the father?"

Edward looked like he wished he'd kept still. "Didn't Nigel say? I'd have thought he couldn't wait."

"What did, uh, Liz think of that?"

"What do you imagine? She couldn't have children herself, and I suppose Abby thought . . ." He shrugged. "Anyway, it doesn't arise because Abby went down to Susan's clinic and terminated. Josef insisted. And once Abby realized how much a child would tie her down, she agreed. At the time I thought it a bit cold blooded of both of them. " He gave me a self-mocking smile. "Like a lot of novelists, I started out with ideals and principles."

Chapter 11

E dward called my hotel around 8:30 the following morning
to say that Josef's former wife would talk to me, but only if
I traveled down to her cottage in Sussex that morning and only
if I brought Abby Russell with me. Since we were already sched-
uled to meet Josef that afternoon, I suggested a different day.
Liz was adamant — it was this morning or never.

Edward was apologetic and so uncomfortable with the situation, he offered to tag along. But when I phoned Abby a few
minutes later, she said no, we'd go alone. Which was interesting. If I'd been facing an interview with the embittered wife of
my former lover, I'd have jumped at the chance of a friendly
buffer. Or remembered a dental appointment in Budapest.

I brushed my teeth in the shower, twisted my hair up on top
of my head with a couple of clips, and managed to be downstairs

when Abby cruised by in a cab. We made the 9:45 train from Victoria Station with minutes to spare.

Victoria to Lewes, in East Sussex, was ninety minutes of lush green countryside blurring past the train windows. It should have been as soothing as a fistful of Xanax, but Mrs. Russell couldn't settle. She crossed her legs, uncrossed them and re-crossed them so often she must have had bruises. If I'd been photographing her for a tabloid, the caption would have read:

Four and a half decades of unresolved guilt.

That reminded me of Edward's pictures. I got them out and asked if she wanted a look. She frowned a no, then changed her mind and shuffled through the faded snapshots three or four times. When she handed them back to me her fingers trembled.

"I wish to God . . ." she began, then stopped, blinked those green eyes and went silent.

I had planned to report on my interviews with Nigel and Edward, but she refused all attempts at conversation or specula-tion as to why Liz had such a burning desire to see her on such short notice. She also refused to ride backward on the train, but I doubted that was a guilt-related issue.

At the Lewes station, we took a cab to Liz's cottage, a white stucco affair with blue shutters, mauve hollyhocks and a sisal door mat. It was all old world and cozy except for a weird mo-ment at the front door when you could hear breathing and knew somebody was standing on the other side not answering.

Eventually the door moved slowly inward and an elderly woman with smooth red hair and a fifty inch waist invited us inside. We followed her through a green and purple sitting room to the back garden where coffee was laid out on a patio table.

Josef's ex was polite to me, but her only interest was Mrs. Russell. Her slightly protuberant eyes took in Abby's face and hair, moved to her raw silk slacks and jacket, noted shoes and jewelry, then returned to the face. If I'd been the recipient of that kind of attention, I'd have made pointed remarks. Abby Russell merely sat, eyes averted, as if waiting for something — perhaps the other shoe — to drop. Or maybe she was just following Steven's orders and trying to clean up some old karma.

Liz was certainly no match for the elegant Josef. Her skin was lumpy, her red lipstick had bled into tiny wrinkles around her mouth and her pink sweatpants could have used an iron.

I sat quietly in the uncomfortable silence, sipped some very good coffee and noted the brandy bottle next to the milk jug without surprise; I'd caught a whiff of Liz's breath on the way to the garden. Next to the brandy, a *Daily Mirror* lay open to a press photo of a well known Hollywood couple canoodling at an A-list party.

Our hostess, who'd apparently stared enough to hold her for a while, turned in her chair and saw me eyeing the article. She shrugged apologetically. "Supermarket sleaze. I got it waiting in line at Waitrose. Astonishing, isn't she?" She waved a hand at the woman in the photograph. "There's her press person working like mad to make her look like Mother Teresa. Adopting third world children, building third world hospitals. And the truth is, she's still a self-absorbed, scheming, husband-stealing cow."

The last five words were delivered in the same off-hand voice as the rest of the remark and followed by a smiling, "Don't mind me. My generation doesn't really understand the young and their staggering sense of entitlement. You probably find nothing wrong with it at all." There was a slight, very slight, emphasis on *you*.

I grinned at her, refusing to be insulted. "With which part? Husband stealing or entitlement?"

Abby Russell got to her feet with an audible breath and settled her purse on her shoulder. "I have to get back to town for a business meeting." She looked at Liz, straight at her for the first time since we'd arrived. "Thanks so much for talking to Keegan. Lovely to see you after all this time. I'll see myself out." And away she went, leaving her coffee untouched on the table. She didn't hurry, and she didn't seem particularly upset — she just went.

I struggled to keep my surprise from showing. A three hour round trip for a six minute encounter? That was it?

Liz smiled as if she'd won some small but important prize, and I wished I was high-tailing it too. There was a dark, heavy feeling about this very ordinary woman that went way beyond losing a few pounds. Still, I was getting paid for sticking it out, assuming she'd talk to me at all now that Abby was gone. I let my eyes drift around the walled-in space of trees, banked flowers, buzzing bees and new-cut grass. "Beautiful garden," I said, with no originality whatever, "very, uh, peaceful."

She nodded, but her eyes stayed in the direction of Abby's retreating back. "I spend a lot of time out here. It's good therapy." A fluffy gray cat with golden eyes appeared on the path, padded over to us and rubbed its chin against her leg, which meant she was probably a good person, basically, unless the cat was her familiar.

At that moment Liz swiveled her head a fast ninety degrees and squinted at me. I barely had time to suppress a shudder when she said, "Well, let's get to it. Edward said you're writing an article about Susan Miachi. What sort of article and why? And, particularly, why now?"

I blocked out memories of *Exorcist* movies, reached for a notebook and quietly switched on the miniature recorder in the bottom of my bag. For some reason, I didn't mind sneaking on Liz.

"It's what I do for a living," I said, shading the truth a couple of degrees, "and it's an interesting story. An American girl gets murdered in 1966 Swinging London, and it's never solved. That's worth a line or two."

She looked unconvinced. "So you interview all Susan's old friends and try to put the pieces together? Fairly useless, I'd think, after all this time. Will we all be featured in the headlines of the prestigious *Sun*, or is this a private affair?"

"I don't write for tabloids, and it's never too late for a story. Sometimes people remember things they didn't realize they knew. Sometimes years later. "

"The sins of the fathers are paid by the sons," she interrupted suddenly, like a character from *Masterpiece Theatre*.

"I beg your pardon?"

"Josef's son, the one called Reid. I never kept track of the others. He won't be pleased, will he? Over Abby turning up, I mean. If you're set to inherit a profitable business, and you learn someone else owns rather a large chunk of it, you tend to get upset." She stretched her neck like a horse. "Well, you do, don't you?"

"You and Josef built up the gallery together, didn't you?"

"Oh, yes, an inspiring story. We met when he came to London in the early fifties. His father had been an artist, and he wanted a gallery of his own. He seemed less like a peasant than a lot of the Hungarians — his features weren't as coarse — and he had a lot of upwardly mobile ideas. I didn't have much money, and he didn't have any at all, but he managed to get in on the ground floor, and we worked all hours for nearly ten years to get established. Then, suddenly, Edgware Road wasn't good enough. We needed a better address, better clientele." She shifted in her chair and shrugged it away. "I can't help you with your story. It was a long time ago. Susan was a very silly girl. Her mother was English — a war bride — but Susan's American upbringing was apparent. She was too friendly with strangers for one thing, always dragging people home or to the gallery, people who weren't the best sort at all."

"You think that's what happened to her? A stranger?"

Her lips pushed out and her eyes narrowed. "The papers said she was married to a crook. Mafia, I think, so I expect that was it. But she worked in that awful birth control clinic, didn't she? Horrible people. Dirty, shiftless lot, passing round the latest exotic diseases."

"What was Susan like besides silly?"

"Any other faceless twenty year old. They all looked alike, you know. She had beautiful clothes, expensive clothes, but Abby ended up with most of them. Talked or traded her out of them. Susan was into Hippie Chic like all the Americans. And naive beyond all comprehension. Always thinking the best of everybody when the evidence showed otherwise. Playing Lady Bountiful, spending her own money to feed those two . . ."

"You mean Nigel and Abby?"

"Of course. And all the while they were blowing what cash they had on drugs and orgies."

"Really." I kept my voice matter of fact and thought she looked disappointed. "But Abby had some money herself. Money she loaned Josef to open the gallery in Chelsea."

"No *loan* about it." Liz reached for the brandy and added a few drops to her coffee. "She handed it over and, of course, that was the end of it. I knew we couldn't afford the move, but he was obsessed. And then she expected to have a say in the way things were done."

"Where did Josef and Abby meet?"

She shook her head. "I never knew where he met any of them. She was just there one day — at the gallery. He had a thing for redheads. God, yes. His mother was one, a famous beauty, supposedly. He had a picture of her in his office, one painted by his father . . ."

The cat jumped suddenly into her lap, and she broke off, tilting her head back into a shaft of sunlight to smile at it. It was an unexpected, loving expression that smoothed out the lines around her mouth and eyes. It was a reminder that she had once been a much younger, more attractive woman. Even her voice was softer. "He married me, but anyone who looked the least bit like Mum could get 'round him."

"And then Abby got pregnant?"

"So she claimed." Her head moved back into the shade. "What does that have to do with your story on Susan?"

"Just trying to fill in the background — get the feel of the Sixties, what they were like."

"The Sixties were about words, and that was the top and bottom of it. Free love, flower power, acid, do your own thing, turn on, drop out, anti-establishment, Carnaby Street." She snorted. "Words. Berlin had the Twenties, Paris the Thirties, and London got stuck with the Sixties. People came to Swinging London from all over the world, but the *movement* was over ten minutes after it started." She glared at me now, as if the decade was all my fault.

"What about the casting off of convention?" I waved a hand. "Being free to live your own life without self-consciousness or guilt?"

"Mere crap from a tiny group of nobodies who smoked dope and screwed everything in sight and got a lot of undeserved publicity. Not one person I knew ever used the word groovy."

"Okay." I shifted in my chair and changed tack. "How and when did you hear about Susan's death?"

"Edward called when they found her body," she said with no

hesitation, "and it was in the papers, of course." Her hand was steady as she poured still another cup of coffee.

"Your husband must have been very upset at the time."

"I don't really remember. We were both away when it happened. We could hardly believe it. Things like that didn't happen to people we knew. It was just more that you never saw her again."

"That's right, Josef was in Europe and you were visiting relatives? Is that right?"

"An aunt." She shrugged. "Two aunts, actually; both dead now. They once owned this cottage."

I nodded. "And Abby took off at the same time, didn't she? Hitchhiked to France and never came back?"

Liz slued her head around again in that odd movement. "That's what she told Edward, at any rate."

"You don't believe it?"

"I expect she just met up with someone wealthier than Josef and did a bunk. You could never be sure; it was whatever Abby wanted at the moment."

"I'm surprised you invited her down today. Considering everything."

"Why not? We've all moved on, and I wondered how she turned out. She's obviously done well, a very high maintenance woman."

"And it doesn't bother you? Seeing her again?"

"Why should it? She really isn't that girl anymore, is she? She's welcome to whatever life she's been able to get for herself."

"Is it possible she discovered Susan's body herself and ran away without telling anyone?"

Liz stared at me for a long, silent moment, lips pushing in and out. "It wouldn't be the Abby I knew," she said finally. "More likely she came back before there *was* a body and that's the real reason she disappeared for forty years."

It took me a second. "You mean *Abby* killed Susan Miachi? Why?"

"Why not? All that rubbish about Susan traveling round the country, seeing Shakespearean plays. She was probably screwing my husband in the back room of some pub."

"You think Susan had an affair with Josef too?"

"Everyone else did." Her face was redder now, either from emotion or brandy. The gray cat stretched and jumped from her lap. It sauntered away, bored by conversation. "Use your head. Susan was pregnant, wasn't she? She wasn't having it off with Edward. Or Nigel, for obvious reasons. Poor Nigel, he doesn't bother pretending any more, but back then it was barely legal." She smirked. "The only other man she knew well was Josef, and with that red hair she was right up his alley."

"And you think Abby was so jealous . . ."

"That little miss was a bitch from day one, and she never went to France or Greece, either. If she'd caught them at it, she'd have beaten that gloating smile right off her face. She was an animal." She stopped mid-rant, breathed through her mouth a couple of times and continued in a thinner voice, "After all these years there won't be any record of who entered or left the country, will there?"

I shook my head. "If she did do it and got away with it, why would she come back now?"

"Well, it's a dead issue, isn't it?" Liz laughed at her own wit. "She's rich now, isn't she? Perhaps returning to the scene of the crime is her idea of fun. Or perhaps she doesn't sleep nights. I wouldn't know." She smoothed her stiff red hair back from her face, adding, "And I really don't care."

Chapter 12

I sat in the buffet car all the way back to town, read the *Daily Mail* and washed down Cadbury chocolate bars with Diet Coke. I needed the sugar. An hour alone with Liz had drained the joy of living right out of my body and made Abby Russell's twenty-something past an even darker, uglier story.

Six people had come together briefly in 1966, and all of them seemed the worse for it: one mysteriously murdered in a basement flat; one in self-exile for forty-six years; one who lived on brandy and bitterness; one who lusted after boys in lederhosen and set his hair on fire.

Edward, I wasn't sure about, unless you counted his two divorces, which wasn't a sign of failure in the new millennium. And Josef? I hadn't heard enough about him to decide. Maybe his antidote to tragedy was simply copper-haired girls young enough to be his granddaughter.

Speaking of Josef, I unwrapped another bar of chocolate and got out my cell phone. Abby had arranged for us to meet him at 3:00, but that was before she ditched out on Liz, and I needed instructions. I punched in numbers, heard her voice say she was unavailable at the moment, and decided I was on my own.

We were supposed to meet for dinner at Rule's in Covent Garden at 8:30. That was probably still on; she had to eat somewhere. If I cabbed straight to the gallery from the station and kept Josef's interview to an hour or so, I could work in a nap before the first course. It had been four days since our arrival, but I still felt a little jet lagged and I wanted to be alert. I had several pertinent questions to ask my employer; questions that were nagging at me:

Why did you leave Liz's house so quickly this morning?

Any chance you killed Susan Miachi yourself and blanked it out for forty years?

Did you and Nigel actually spend all your money on drugs and orgies in the Sixties?

Did you really have an abortion?

I wanted to watch her eyes when she answered to see when and if she dissembled.

Or just plain lied.

All of this was a reasonable plan, but only the nap part worked out. For one thing, Josef was a no-show, and the gallery was locked up tight. For another, when I arrived at Rule's for dinner at 8:25, Abby Russell obviously had a program of her own.

"Edward's joining us. I hope you don't mind," she murmured as the waiter led us to a table for four. She had redone her makeup, but it didn't cover the dark gray smudges around her eyes. She looked exhausted and depressed. It was probably a poor time for questions. On the other hand, once Edward arrived, questions would be impossible.

"No, that's fine," I said, "but I would like to ask about Liz before he gets here. Was she always so strange?"

"It's hard to say." Abby sat up straighter. "She was always so afraid of losing Josef, I never knew what she was really like."

"And you didn't help matters?"

For a moment there was silence, then she nodded. "Quite right, I didn't help."

"Oddly enough, she didn't seem bitter toward you."

"The husband stealing cow?"

"Even then, there wasn't much heat behind it. She just wanted to look at you, or so she said."

Abby pushed a few red-gold strands of hair behind one ear. "Did she say anything important after I left?"

"Not really. She was in the country visiting her aunts and didn't find out about Susan's murder until the day after it happened. She couldn't remember if Josef was upset, and none of it seemed real. That kind of stuff." I eyed her across the table. "There was one interesting thing, though."

"What's that?"

"She thinks you might have done it."

"You're joking. She actually said that?"

"She said Susan and Josef were having an affair, and it was his baby."

"That's a stupid lie, and she knows it!"

I shrugged and looked at the menu. Rule's was the oldest restaurant in London and famous for locally grown game. Not that I knew that firsthand; I'd spent my hard earned money on fish and chips rather than red deer loin, even in prosperous years. The special today appeared to be roast saddle of braised Wiltshire rabbit.

Wonderful. Where was pepperoni pizza when you really needed it?

"She also said you had an abortion yourself," I added, without looking up. "You didn't mention that."

"No." Her voice was still angry. "What else?"

"That you and Nigel were heavily into drugs and group sex back then. That she doesn't know who killed Susan and doesn't care." I leaned back in my chair. "But maybe she does know and just doesn't care. Maybe Josef did it and that's why they split up."

Abby's face was a frowning mask. "You can't go by what she says. She was always getting at you, insinuating things. Like she really didn't *know* anything, but wasn't it *odd*? Jerking people around for the fun of it. Why else insist that we see her today or not at all? Her way or the highway."

"Strange lady." I repeated. "It's surprising that Edward continues to see her."

'He's sorry for her, I guess. She was actually a very pretty girl. Stylish, really. Edward thinks she got a raw deal. He's a very kind man."

"Kinder than Nigel, apparently, who didn't even know where she lived."

She picked up her menu. "Nigel hasn't seen her since the day it happened, according to Edward. He was — such a nice boy back then, Nigel. Warm, funny, excited about everything. Never . . . waspish."

"Neither he nor Liz has worn very well."

"I guess not, but not for the same reason. Or," she sighed. "maybe it was. Edward says nothing was the same after — after Susan. Nigel moved away and wasn't heard from for a year or more. Josef left the running of the gallery to Liz for months, then moved his clothes out one day without a word. Edward thinks Josef blamed her. For me going away, I mean."

"Is that right? Was Liz the reason you fled the country?"

She gave me a half-amused, half-sarcastic look. "Please. Do you honestly remember why you did anything at all when you were twenty?"

"Yeah, it was always sex," I said.

Her mouth opened slightly. "I'm sorry."

"I was a product of my generation. Nearly all my missteps were directly linked to sex."

Her green eyes looked slightly less tired. "Interesting choice of words. Missteps as in blunders? Lapses in judgment? Bad moves? Where I grew up it was just plain sin. There were only two kinds, and venial didn't count. Misstep is more comfortable, I suppose. No guilt trip."

I softened and grinned. I liked her better the longer I was around her; especially when the thoughtful, mildly sarcastic woman peered out from behind the moneyed, victimized facade. I wondered if she'd always been difficult to know or if she'd learned to keep people at arms' length. Maybe internment in the hippie camp for three years had taught her hard lessons.

"Oh, the guilt gets you eventually," I assured her. "Its just not your mother's immobilizing, take-the-veil kind of guilt. More the take-a-Zoloft kind." I waved the menu in her direction. "I still get flashbacks."

"Flashbacks? Really?"

I nodded with a straight face. "Every time they play 'Get Outta My Dreams, Get Into My Car', I remember dancing on bars or skinny dipping in the neighbor's pool or smoking marijuana or other stuff. I wasn't a serious danger to public morals, but those weren't my finest hours."

Abby Russell leaned back, elbows on her chair arms, a half-smile on her pale face. "So many old memories are just silly. Embarrassing and kind of sad. Best released and forgotten."

"True." I looked at the menu and wondered if I could manage the rabbit pie. "Of course, the stuff we did back then wouldn't raise any eyebrows now. Mention guilt to today's teenagers and they say, 'How do you spell that? G-i-l-t?' "

She propped her chin on one hand. "But there's always that one thing you wish you'd done differently. God, you'd think you'd just grow out of it after a while." She broke off as the waiter approached. "Still, Steven says you can only improve the present. How about a very large drink? I understand they're famous for Bellinis here."

"Good idea. I don't think I can eat a bunny without one."

When the waiter left to fill our order, she leaned toward me. "How was your meeting with Josef?"

"He wasn't there, surprise, surprise. I called later and talked to a girl on the desk. She swears he'll be in at eleven tomorrow, but I think he's sandbagging until we leave town."

"Oh, he'll see you eventually. To protect his investment, if nothing else." Her voice was brittle. "It's all money in the end, isn't it?"

I opened my mouth to ask how much of the gallery she actually owned and if she planned to claim a portion, but closed it when I saw Edward crossing the room toward us.

From the second he sat down and took in Abby's drawn face, Edward put himself out to be entertaining. As we drank the most expensive fresh peach and champagne cocktails of my experience, he avoided any mention of our trip to see Liz. Instead he talked about theater, politics, art and his new project — the East African drought. Edward, it appeared, was resurrecting the ghost of his dead writing career, this time in the form of a documentary. He'd also been raising money to build wells and water treatment plants in Somali villages for the past two years.

Mrs. Russell's tired face smoothed out after her second drink, and she listened with flattering attention to his descriptions of heat and poverty and suffering. She said she'd always wanted a career in journalism and encouraged him to continue working on the documentary, no matter what the obstacles. I thought she was laying it on a little thick, but maybe it was just what she knew how to do. After the third round of Bellinis I had a psychic flash, a flash that said if nobody else funded his masterpiece, Abby Russell would be standing by, checkbook in hand.

All in all, it was a relaxing, stimulating two hours with no mention of Susan Miachi and/or murder. By the time we left Rule's and walked down the street to a small dark bar for a nightcap, it was obvious to me that Abby and Edward were rekindling whatever fire they'd been playing with back in 1966.

On the way home in my solitary cab, I reached for my cell phone, then realized it was five a.m. in Florida. Too early literally to call Sunni and too early figuratively to suggest Edward or Josef as a likely father. Not Nigel. Nigel probably wasn't in the equation. I settled back in the seat and wished I'd stopped drinking three drinks ago. And then an interesting thought found its way into my foggy brain. If Nigel hadn't seen Liz since the late Sixties, how had he managed to give me such an up-to-date physical description of her?

The morning after, I woke up just in time to shower, throw on some jeans and flag down a cab for Chelsea. It was gray and nasty and pouring down rain, a perfect day to stay in bed and baby my hangover. I French braided my hair in the taxi, debated stopping on the way for aspirin, decided against it, since I was determined to catch Josef the second he opened for business, and vowed never again to mix three Bellinis with two brandy and sodas.

At six minutes past eleven, I presented my rain soaked self and a pounding headache at the Gallery on Jubilee Walk. Once again, I struck out.

". . . terribly sorry, he's running a bit late . . . emergency telephone call from Germany." The girl at the desk regarded my half-mast eyes with a mixture of uneasiness and curiosity. "He's usually here by now. Would you like a mug of tea while you wait?"

"Never mind, Lorna, I'll take care of her."

I looked up as Reid, the wonder son, strolled into the room. He was wearing jeans and a Steelers baseball cap turned backward on his head, and he still needed a shave.

"Come back," he said to me, "and I'll give you a coffee." He turned and went as if disobeying wasn't an option, and I let my desperate need for caffeine override my irritation at being ordered around.

As we passed through Beijing's display of art work, I noticed several blank spaces and stopped to see what was missing.

"Somebody bought the cross full of sins?" I said, astonished.

Reid made an affirmative noise. "A friend of my father's."

"The headless paintings are gone too. Every one."

"Didn't Mrs. Russell tell you? She bought them all the day after the opening."

In the back office Reid filled an electric kettle with water, plugged it in and reached for a jar of instant coffee. "Sugar? Cream?"

"Neither, thanks."

He spooned black powder into two mugs. "Nigel says you're not only a journalist, you're a surfer. You look pretty substantial for a wave jumper. Don't surfers drop out, live in vans and say things like 'gnarly'?"

"It isn't a life calling." I rubbed the back of my neck and refused to be baited. "I only learned how last year." I glanced out the window at the rain. "And would I rather be surfing at this moment than sitting here? Absolutely."

The arrogant expression shifted to something like amusement. "We've got some painkillers around here somewhere. Want one with your coffee?"

"An aspirin would be great."

"I'm sorry my father's not around to answer questions." He placed the two mugs on the table and rummaged in a drawer. "Maybe you'd like to take a crack at me so your trip won't be a total loss."

"Why?" I looked at the kettle which was taking its sweet time boiling. "You weren't around forty years ago."

"Nearly. Thirty-seven."

I was six years older. I calculated it quickly, although I'm notoriously bad at math and didn't care anyway.

"Consider the situation," he continued in a musing voice. "Mystery woman returns after many years, journalist in tow, to suss out her American friend's death. Journalist interviews people in American friend's old circle, which is quite small, really, possibly trying to discover if one of them murdered aforementioned girl or knows who did. And mystery woman is shoved in front of a taxi rather early in the game."

"How do you know she was shoved?"

He gave me a look that said my head wasn't working. "Everybody standing out front heard her say so. Anyway, as the son who inherits the gallery, which may be partially owned by said mystery woman, I consider myself someone who merits attention. Not as much attention as my father, of course, who knew the departed only too well. Or as much as Liz, his first wife, who retains an interest and hates encroachers like poison. But it would obviously be to my benefit if mystery woman departed quickly with all questions unanswered about an unfortunate death four decades ago. Bad publicity for one thing, one less to share with for another, and there's always the chance I'm privy to someone's old and possibly criminal secrets."

"I suppose," I began slowly. Then: "What do you mean *retains an interest*? Liz has money in the gallery too?"

"Certainly," he pushed his cap back off his forehead, "the one on Edgware Road was in her name. She refused to let my father buy her out, and for some reason he never insisted. He pays her a percentage. Has for years."

Really?

Maybe Liz was hanging around the night of the opening, protecting her interests, and gave Abby Russell a tiny shove.

No, of course not. I needed caffeine worse than I thought. There was no way she'd have known who Abby was at that point or even that she was in London.

I shifted my gaze back to Reid. "So, if you know all about it, who did kill Susan Miachi?"

He gave me the smug smile again. "Her Mafia husband or someone he hired to track her down?"

"It appears he didn't," I said.

"How do you know? Because he said so?"

Because some California psychic said so. I kept that thought to myself.

He placed two powdery white pills in the palm of my hand. "The real question is, does dear Abby actually believe one of the old crowd offed her friend, or is she just getting even with my father for something that happened a long time ago?"

I shrugged. "Don't forget, she left him."

"True. And according to my mother — ex-wife number two — he never got over it."

"He was that smitten?"

"Apparently. Though some say if you've bedded one red-head, you've bedded them all. Our Henry the Eighth, for one."

"So cynical for thirty-seven years."

"I acquired it honestly. What kind of questions did you intend to ask my father?"

"Oh, I don't know, the usual. Where he was when he heard about Susan's death. Does he know who might have done it. Did he actually have an affair with her as someone suggested."

The kettle began to blow out steam, and Reid poured boiling water into the two cups.

"If you wash both tablets down with very hot coffee, you'll feel better almost immediately."

"Where'd you learn that?"

"Wharton School, actually."

"University of Pennsylvania?"

"The very one."

"I had you pegged for a rocker."

"Was. Once." He grinned all over his face. "My father gave me two years to make it or get it out of my system. It was brilliant. Yet, here I am."

I swallowed the pills gingerly with scalding coffee, in spite of the warnings programmed into my DNA about strangers and drugs. Wharton graduates don't poison people, right? I looked up at him. "Why business school?"

"A compromise. My father embraces all things English. He'd have preferred Sandhurst or Cambridge, London School of Economics at the very least." He shrugged and dropped it. "It affected his whole life, you know. The death. Abby leaving. I didn't know for years that she helped fund the new gallery, not until Nigel let it slip. I suppose technically she's still a partner."

"You'd have to ask her. It doesn't sound like there was anything in writing, and I don't think she needs the money."

"No, I suppose not." After a long moment he looked away. "She's not nearly the wild child I'd been led to expect. Are you free tonight by any chance?"

The change of topic caught me by surprise. "I — I'm not sure."

"When do you think you'll be sure?"

I took another mouthful of coffee, blessed drug of choice, and decided I was feeling better. "Mrs. Russell may have something planned. I am working, you know. This is a working trip."

"Of course. It's just that there's an opening in the East End tonight, and my father will be there early on. You could come with me and interview him in a more relaxed — for him — situation."

"I thought I was interviewing him this morning."

Reid glanced at his watch. "I'm guessing there's been another emergency, and he won't be in after all."

I sipped coffee and considered the offer. "I don't understand why you'd help me get to him. What do you have against your father?"

"Nothing, just my slightly decadent, ambiguous sense of what's appropriate. I'm a very ambiguous guy. Can't help myself."

When I didn't say anything, he looked up and shrugged. "I learned several things from my mother. One was that avoiding the truth never works. Better to face and finish it."

"Do you know specifically what he's trying to avoid?"

He shook his head. "He's never said. And I don't ask."

At that moment the girl from the front desk peeked through the open office door.

"I'm terribly sorry, Ms. Shaw," she said, "but Josef won't be coming in after all. Unavoidable emergency. He says perhaps another time."

Chapter 13

The rain had stopped by the time Reid picked me up at the hotel that night. He arrived in a black, late model BMW, and except for faded blue jeans, he matched the car perfectly: black T-shirt, black leather jacket, black trainers. I was wearing a pale green silk sweater dress I'd picked up at Selfridges that afternoon. It hugged most of my good parts in most of the right places, kept me warm and allowed me to shun gallery black as a matter of principle.

I had phoned Abby Russell from the department store, admitted missing Josef again, and invited her to join us at the gallery opening. She said it would be better if I spoke to him alone and reported later. I also phoned daughter Sunni and left similar information on her voice mail. Then, duties fulfilled, I bought a pair of heels to match the new dress, gave myself

a really lavish tea in the restaurant and went back to the hotel
to crawl in bed. New clothes, hot crumpets dripping with Irish
butter, and blessed sleep. *Is this living or what?* I thought, as I
sunk into the pillows.

Reid was a good driver, I guess. He changed lanes often and
braked even oftener for the buses, bicycles and pedestrians that
popped up in front of us like an obstacle course. After a while
I realized we probably weren't going to hit anyone, settled back
into the BMW's glove-leather bucket seat and watched London literally flash by: Bloomsbury, Holborn, the City, Hoxton,
Shoreditch. There was probably no better way to arrive at what
the *London Times* had referred to, that very morning, as "the
Edgy East End art scene."

In my photography days, condos and trendy restaurants
were shooting up all over the Docklands, but people stayed
away from Hoxton or Spitalfields or Bethnal Green unless they
were starving artists or seriously slumming. Now the Edgy East
End was obviously the place to be.

"Dozens of small galleries around here," Reid said, as he
wedged the BMW into a tiny space between a Bentley and a
brick wall, "but this is one of the best. The economy hasn't
helped, but there's still international money here, enough to get
on with, at least."

"I thought Islington was the hot spot."

"Used to be, but it got too expensive and too gentrified. All
the YBAs moved over into Hoxton. YBAs don't mind grungy
council flats and the occasional rat."

"Young British Artists?"

"Very good." He unfastened his seat belt. "Anyway, here
we are — B&W, Bang and Whimper, formerly a block of tottery

council houses. Named by a frustrated T.S. Eliot fan I expect, or an S&M *aficionado*. It's an insider's warehouse now, completely staffed and funded by teaching artists. Nigel has some money in it. We'll likely see him here."

Reid got out of the car and came around to open the passenger door. "Careful, there's not much room for you to climb out. I don't want you to bruise your . . . er, dress."

I swung my legs sideways, sucked in my stomach and edged up into the six inch gap left by the open car door.

Reid put a hand on my left hip and another behind my right shoulder. "Arms up," he ordered, and I held both hands high as he pulled me carefully in his direction." His breath was warm on my neck.

"Parking anywhere these days is nearly impossible," he murmured, nudging the door shut with one knee. For a moment we stood together in the narrow space. He'd apparently shaved for the occasion and his smooth face was so close it blurred. Heat was either emerging from his body to engulf mine, or I was having an early hot flash. I took a Zen-like breath and sidled sideways. I'm not good in small, tight places. "Is your father here?"

"Already inside. See the white stretch limo across the street? He likes being chauffeured. He can stay glued to his mobile phone and baby sit Beijing at the same time." He took my arm and aimed us at the door. "Practical, rather than warm and cuddly, my dad, but he did give me my philosophy of life. He and Georgie Best."

"Best? The soccer player?"

"The soccer legend."

"I stand corrected. What philosophy is that?"

He cocked an eyebrow at me. "As Georgie said once, when asked, 'I spent a lot of money on booze, birds and fast cars. The rest I squandered.' "

I laughed out loud.

A lean, mean male body is always interesting, but one attached to a dry sense of humor gets to me faster than three Bellinis on an empty stomach. For half a second I thought of dragging Reid back to the car and doing serious damage to my new dress, then I breathed in and blinked the thought away. I'm also not good in wrinkled clothes. For all I knew, parking in cramped, intimate spaces might be a carefully honed dating technique.

"Business first." He leaned down as if he'd read my mind and kissed the corner of my mouth. "We can sort out our bottom lines later. After a polite quarter hour, Josef will be looking for the nearest exit and shouting, 'Where are the paintings? I thought galleries had paintings!' "

Inside the B&W Gallery, Reid steered me down a long narrow corridor made of old doors lashed together with rope. The corridor, someone's historically inspired art work, was titled Roman Bridge, and it swayed under our feet. Giant blue lava lamps marked the entrance to the vast, scruffy, open space of the gallery itself. The lamps threw out an eerie, wavering light, and you could almost imagine yourself back in 43 AD, crossing London's first makeshift raft-bridge amidst the sounds of clanking armor and Latin swear words.

"Computerized light pieces," Reid explained when he saw me studying the lamps. "My father finds them objectionable, but he thinks all these galleries a bit dodgy. That's the point, of course. When you're paying significantly lower rent, you take more risks."

At that moment I spotted Josef standing beneath an enormous, twenty-foot orange clock painted on a free-standing wall. With him was a short, coffee-colored woman in a yellow jumpsuit. Josef's crisp gray hair, dark eyes and still-rugged jaw made him look like an old time movie actor who'd gone slumming. His voice, however, was pedantic, slightly testy and became louder as we crossed the room.

". . . paintings were once the rage with the hedge-fund crowds, but the prices for his work have plummeted over the last year. No one is doing well, and anyone who says they are is lying, but we're a deep-pockets gallery. Anyway, things were considerably grimmer in the early Nineties. I've no patience with . . ."

"The woman he's speaking to is the best trash trawler in the business," Reid murmured to me. "You call it dumpster diving in the U.S. She's scrounged scrap metal from Istanbul to Geneva. Owns a warehouse full of fabulous stuff — even a crack den from Mexico City."

"You're kidding. She travels the world collecting garbage?"

"She does ship the exceptional bits home, but usually she creates *in situ.*" He lowered his voice. "The lecture is winding down, I think. When she moves away, I'll introduce you properly. Talk fast, while Beijing's not around."

"Where is Beijing?"

"Upstairs, I imagine. Her former boyfriend lives here." He led me toward Josef as the trash trawler moved away. "They spend a certain amount of time every week — uh — reconnecting. I'd say you've got twenty minutes tops."

I was willing to talk fast, but I never got a chance. After Reid introduced us and moved away, Josef segued from so nice to see you again to Art World 101 discourse without drawing a breath. He'd have made a dandy filibusterer, if there is such a word.

" . . . people who are frantic about the economy . . . I say it's a godsend. A chance for people to remember that the best art is still in Piccadilly and Mayfair, an opportunity to chop away the dead wood of would-be artists who've grown fat on entitlement and government subsi . . ."

I tried to keep my eyes from watering. Abby Russell had been right to stay home, although at the time I thought she was just wimping out. After all, she had collapsed when she first saw her ex-lover with Beijing, and I had doubted the low blood sugar story. It was possible that she'd planned to reconnect with Josef after her husband's death and the sight of him connected to someone thirty years younger was too much to handle. Especially if the detectives she hired had failed to mention Beijing's presence.

I swallowed another yawn and decided Abby was better off without him. Josef might have been a hot ticket in 1966, but four decades and a half later he was a heart-stopping boor.

I stared at the giant orange clock on the wall behind him. Its second hand, a long gold phallus-like shape, dangled oddly between the 3 and the 4. I looked again. It *was* a phallus, a huge one. As it reached the six, which was actually a 6 and a 9 intertwined, it sproinged out into a long, stiff — whoa! How the hell did they manage that? Inspired, I stiffened my resolve, shifted my eyes to Reid's father and interrupted without apology.

"It's fascinating, the London art scene, but tell me a little about Susan Miachi. Would she have been a great talent today?"

Josef's eyes seemed to glaze over, then focused somewhere around my left ear. For a second I thought he wouldn't answer. "She certainly had a unique way of looking at things," he said at last. "It would depend on how she developed, of course. In New York, for example . . ."

I averted a foray into U.S. art scene by demanding, "Who hated her enough to kill her?"

The dark eyes moved to the right, then back to my ear again as he took in a steadying breath. "No one hated Susan. The Sixties were a time of turmoil, and London had its share of thefts and break-ins. She was often too friendly, being American, I suppose, and possibly gave someone the wrong idea. Always bringing new people — sometimes even foreigners she'd met — to the gallery . . . and to Nigel's flat, I believe."

"So, she just got in the way of an attempted robbery? What about her husband? The Mafia don or whatever."

"Yes, of course, I'd forgotten. So long ago. I seem to remember hearing she'd run away, and he found her."

"It must have been a surprise to see Abby again. Have you had a chance to get together? To talk?" I gave him an innocent smile.

"No, not really. Perhaps when the show is finished," he said, adjusting the cuffs on his immaculate shirt.

"Is she still a partner in the gallery? Technically?"

"Abby was never a partner *per se*." He looked pained or annoyed, I wasn't sure which. "She helped out many years ago when I was moving to a larger space, but the amount of money involved was not remarkable. When she disappeared so suddenly I had no idea where to send further payments and after a time —" He lifted a hand and let it drop. "Some sort of accounting could be made, although I understand that she — Abby — is quite a wealthy woman in her own right." The words came smoothly, but his voice was a little strained. "A small thing to her, I expect."

"Josef? Darling?" Beijing, flushed and nearly breathless, materialized beside him, the smell of marijuana or burning marjoram floating out of her clothes. Her eyes narrowed as she recognized me. She snaked an arm around Josef's waist and pressed a large, barely covered breast into his ribs. "I don't believe we've met," she said.

Josef grew at least an inch and a half taller. "Keegan Shaw, darling. A friend of Reid's. We were just discussing art in general, actually."

She stared at me, eyes over-bright and mildly spiteful. "Keegan. That's Irish, isn't it? A boy's name, though, really. Isn't it? Keegan?" She stretched out the long ee's.

I nodded. "Yep. Beijing's unusual too. You don't look Chinese."

"Certainly not." Her smug look turned icy. "Come, Josef," She took his arm and turned her back on Reid as he came to join us. "I'm feeling peckish. We can discuss the gallery's new direction while we eat." She emphasized new, as if she'd underlined it, and pulled Josef away before he could say anything else. It didn't seem to bother him much.

I grinned at Reid. "Oops, too late. They've gone. She seems a little touchy about her name. Is there a back story?"

"There is." He took my arm and moved us away from the orange clock.

"She was really Noreen Lloyd, a fabulously mediocre Welsh watercolorist who came up to London with her boyfriend and formed a ménage-a-something with a landscape artist named Sho Shu. Sho Shu was thought to be a woman. When the three fell out, Noreen took a pair of shears to Shu's wardrobe and nailed it to the bathroom wall. Then she spray painted a four letter word beginning with C across the lot over and over — in red."

"Seems a bit drastic."

Reid shook his head. "That's not the best part. The boyfriend removed the bathroom wall intact, titled it Red Army, signed the name Beijing across it in the same red paint and peddled it to a gallery in Hoxton. A Russian businessman bought it for five figures and the story made the Sun and the Daily Mail. Then the art magazines jumped on it, and there you have it — birth of a new talent."

"And she and the boyfriend still speak?"

"Of course, they're artists. She'll return to him when she

tires of Josef. Unless," his smile tightened a little, "she talks Papa into marrying her and snakes the gallery out from under me. She's lasted a bit longer than the others."

"But your father — surely he knows. Is she a whiz at business or something?"

"She doesn't know market upturn from short-term flood. She only knows that the big buyers are Russians or Asians with second homes in England. Still, she talked him into her strange and wonderful opening, and he's not known for challenging new art, let alone dramatic overstatement."

"Interesting." I thought it over. "So, if something happened to your dad, and she and the boyfriend edged you out, then only Abby would still have a share of the gallery?"

"There's always Liz."

"Oh, yes, I forgot. I'd check on her periodically, if I were you. If Abby gets mowed down by a taxi, Liz might be the next to go."

Reid led me farther into the depths of the warehouse to look at the Big Box art for which Bang and Whimper was famous. One exhibit, titled Starter Home, consisted of a depressing expanse of bare cement floor, partially painted walls, gigantic ornate mirrors, draped blood-red sheets and broken metal chairs.

The small crowd surrounding the display included Nigel and a tall bony woman, possibly the artist, who were deep in discussion.

"It may seem laughably slight at first," the woman was saying, waving a cigarette in the air, "but at second look one gets a sense of poignancy, a longing for human contact that goes beyond."

"She's kidding, right?" I whispered to Reid.

He gave me a sideways grin. "Don't you long for human contact after looking at it?"

"That or assisted suicide."

Nigel spotted us, glanced from Reid to me with a half smile, and waved us over. He introduced us to the woman, but I lost most of her name and pertinent information in the surrounding noise.

" . . . darling Carmela . . . the Arts Council . . . lavish coffee table book . . . you're nobody if you don't have one . . . based in Germany . . . huge smash with her Total Crap series." He peered at me. "You remember the Birdshit paintings?"

I shook my head.

The woman rolled her eyes and moved away, apparently to find someone who did.

Nigel took my arm. "I'll entertain Keegan. Go find us drinks and something to eat. Hopefully this plague of locusts hasn't devoured everything."

Reid disappeared in a wave of bodies, and Nigel and I looked each other over. He was dressed down tonight in sharply pressed jeans, a tank top and corduroy jacket and he looked all business. I decided I preferred the red leisure suit.

"What is it you actually do?" I said to him. "Promotion? Fund raising?"

He nodded. "Yes. I'm also installation coordinator, technical designer and project assistant. Even been known to appraise on occasion. Keep the wolf from the door, that's the ticket." He smiled and cocked his head to one side. "What are you doing here?"

"You invited me."

"I didn't know you'd come with Reid."

"Josef's been avoiding me. Reid offered to arrange an interview if I came to the opening tonight."

"Josef's here?"

"Standing under the giant orange clock."

"How appropriate," Nigel murmured. "And did you have your nice talk?"

"Yes, but I didn't learn anything useful."

"No, I suppose not." He had stopped listening and was frowning at a girl who'd begun painting one of Starter Home's bare gray walls with what looked like a dripping yellow broom. "Not so tentative, Elsa," he called to her. "It's performance art. Large, passionate strokes, darling. If it looks bad later, we'll just repaint; it's not like a vasectomy."

"So," he turned back to me, "where's our Abby tonight? Still discussing the past with old friends? Like Edward or possibly Liz?"

"She's at the hotel as far as I know. Speaking of Liz, how did you know what she looks like these days? I thought you hadn't seen her since Susan Miachi died."

Nigel raised an eyebrow. "Don't ask trick questions, darling, you're no good at it. Liz was in town a few weeks ago lunching in Neal Street with Edward. I ducked out the back way to be honest. I didn't recognize her at first with that horrible blonde hair, which I suppose she thinks makes her look younger."

"She had red hair when I saw her."

"Wigs. She had cancer a while back. Edward said her hair came back all gray and spidery." He shuddered. "Red on her is criminal, but blonde makes her look like a menopausal Barbie doll."

"Liz thinks Josef was the father of Susan Miachi's baby."

Nigel waved Liz's thought processes away with one hand. "It wouldn't be the first time she thought she heard voices, and it was only the Hoover."

A loud shrill ring interrupted us. I looked around to see what it was before realizing it came from my clutch purse.

"Sorry," I fished the cell phone out and glanced at the display. "I think I'd better take this." I smiled an apology at the trite phrase and walked a few feet away. "Hello?"

"Keegan, it's Abby Russell." Her voice was shaking, and I could barely understand the words.

"What's the matter? Are you all right?" The noise level was so high I had to shout to hear myself.

"Yes. No. I can't . . . somebody left a package for me at the desk. I had them bring it up here."

"Is it ticking? Should we call the police?"

She ignored my attempt at humor. "It's a scrapbook of cuttings. Newspaper cuttings. All about Susan's death. All in order . . . all old and yellow and horribly, horribly in order." Her voice shuddered to a halt."I'm sorry, but if you could . . ."

"Okay, okay. Put it under the bed and don't look at it until I get there."

Chapter 14

I talked Reid into staying at the gallery with Nigel. "No point in spoiling your evening," I said as I got into the taxi.

"Too late." He leaned down to look in at me. "You haven't even had a drink. I don't understand why she's freaked out over a book of newspaper cuttings."

"I told you. They're about Susan Miachi. After saving them for forty years, somebody decided to dump them on her twenty minutes ago. Good night. Thanks for —"

He leaned further into the cab, kissed my mouth medium hard and slid a business card into my hand. "That's my mobile number. Call me later if you get free. I stay up late." Then he gave the driver a twenty pound note, closed the taxi door and watched as we pulled away from the curb. It was at least ten blocks before the feel of his mouth went away.

At the Abbott Hotel, I went straight to a house phone and asked to be connected to Abby Russell. She answered on the third ring, whispered her room number, and I took an elevator to the sixth floor.

Mrs. Russell had made herself at home in one of the Abbott's chi chi suites. A pair of bronze heels lay on the pale blue carpet, two thick bottomed tumblers sat on a low coffee table, and a leather purse had been upended atop the white sofa. The scrapbook, dusty black buckram, was totally out of place in the elegant sitting room. It lay on the floor between a tiny backlit bar and a cream tiled electric fireplace. Bits of packaging were scattered around it.

Abby let me in only after demanding, "Who is it?" several times, in a panicky voice, then fled to the white sofa and left me to lock the corridor door. The French doors between the bedroom and sitting room were standing open, and I could see a blue silk bedspread crumpled in a pile on the floor. The smell of expensive perfume drifted in the air.

Abby herself looked less elegant than usual. She was wrapped in a pale blue blanket and shaking so badly her teeth made clicking sounds. I've seen scared, and once I saw terrorized, but this was something different, something old and ugly and helpless.

Flames were leaping and flickering behind the fireplace's glass front, but they didn't make the suite any warmer. I picked up one of the tumblers, carried it to the bar and filled it with brandy. Then I came back and wedged the glass in her trembling fingers. "Here, this'll warm you up, stop the shaking."

For a second irritation displaced the look of fear. "I'm not an alcoholic, if that's what you think, in spite of what I drank on the plane."

"Just get it down. How can a scrapbook make you crazy?"

She closed her eyes and moved her head back and forth. "The minute I opened it a whole lot of bad karma just came up out of it like fog. It was like I was actually there — in the flat — and she was dead. All red carpet and disgusting smells — and no air to breathe at all." She shuddered and the glass wobbled. "And while I was standing here holding the clippings, trying to calm down, there was a scrabbling sound at my door. Like somebody trying to get in. I was — it was terrifying. I grabbed my phone and locked myself in the bathroom and rang you up. I didn't come out 'til you knocked."

"You sure it wasn't the maid?"

"The maid has a key." She lifted the glass with shaky hands and buried her nose in brandy.

"Well, let's take a look." I walked over and picked up the black book.

"You look." She downed the brandy, shivered and pulled the blanket closer.

The scrapbook had originally been a photograph book. Its thick gray pages were nearly as yellow as the newspaper clippings glued to them. The first article was the same one Mrs. Russell had showed me on the plane. The next three were from different papers and dated the following day. After that there were clippings every day for weeks. Most of them were the same: information about the dead girl; interviews with neighbors; a report that Susan Miachi had been pregnant; an interview with Nigel after he returned from Spain; and an appeal for Abby Pell, believed to be traveling in the Midlands, to contact police at her earliest convenience.

There was only one picture of Susan Miachi. It looked like she'd been cropped out of Edward's photo of the four of them in front of Big Ben. Several days later, there was another appeal for Abby Pell or anyone who knew her whereabouts to contact police.

"They must not have checked with passport control," I said, "or they'd have known you were in France."

She grunted and closed her eyes. "Who kept these? And why give them to me?"

"I don't know," I muttered and kept reading.

Eventually the dates got farther and farther apart. Police reported that the dead girl was married to an Anthony Miachi of Cranston, Rhode Island, who was linked to New England crime leaders. His wife Susan had disappeared several months earlier while he was in jail on an arson charge. Another article said police could find no evidence that Anthony Miachi had ever entered England.

The last item was an interview with a neighbor, at 156 Finborough Road, who said her heart had nearly stopped when she found there were Mafia people living in the building next door — and it was no wonder her milk so often went missing from the front step.

There was a picture of the woman pointing at the door of 146 with her other hand held to her throat. The photographer had done a good job. The woman's eyes were bulging, but she didn't look frightened. She looked like it was the most exciting day of her life.

I went through the clippings again, this time looking for facts and found four:

1) An anonymous telephone call to a police substation had come in a little after a quarter of three on the afternoon Susan died. The voice was believed to be male.

2) Police arrived at 146 Finborough Road shortly afterward and discovered the body and evidence of a fire.

3) The fire had started in a metal dust bin placed next

to the body in the lounge and had charred part of a tablecloth and some of deceased's clothing before burning itself out in the damp carpet.

4) The body was identified by Edward Mowery, who lived upstairs in the first floor flat.

I read the item about the anonymous caller again and turned to Abby. "I kind of thought it was you."

"What was me?" She was now only shuddering every couple of minutes.

"I thought you found Susan's body and called the police from the tube station. I thought that was why you disappeared."

"I didn't call." Her troubled eyes looked into mine. "No."

"No." I laid the book down on a coffee table. "It was a man's voice, and there are only three men involved. Nigel was in Spain so it must have been Edward or Josef."

'Not Edward. He'd never handle it that way."

"Josef, then? Is that why you're avoiding him? Did Josef kill her?"

"I don't know. But I think somebody sent me this book as a warning to keep my nose out. And who was scratching on my door tonight? Who would do that?"

"There's no reason for anybody to threaten you," I said in my most calming voice, "unless you know something you're not supposed to know. Sure you weren't around that day? Didn't see somebody?"

Her head was shaking before I finished. "No — honestly."

"Maybe the scratcher was Edward, and he just dropped by without calling. He knows your room number, right?"

"Yes, but the desk didn't call about the scrapbook until after he left. "We met for dinner," she explained off-handedly, "and he came up here for a while after."

Ah. That would explain the silk blanket crumpled on the bedroom floor. "Well, if it was Josef or Nigel, they were awfully quick about it. I just saw both of them at the gallery."

"Oh?" The thought distracted her for a moment. "What did Josef have to say for himself?"

"He said it was actually a very small amount of money you lent him years ago, and he paid some of it back."

Her face went from pale to bright scarlet. "Oh, really? It was eight thousand pounds. He never returned a dime."

I shrugged and grinned at her. "Look, we're kind of dead-ended here. There's nobody left to talk to. You honestly don't know anything you haven't told me?"

"No, nothing that — nothing. I thought — when I saw them all again — I thought somebody would know what really happened and just didn't say. I didn't know it would all be up to me. I have to talk to Steven. I wish to God I'd just stayed home and . . ."

"Had nightmares?"

She flashed me an angry look. "You can't even imagine . . ." She waved a hand at the scrapbook. "Take that thing with you. Please. I don't want it in my room. I'll call you tomorrow after I've had time to think. I'll still pay you. I just have to think about it."

I picked up the clippings along with my purse. "Are you going to be all right by yourself? You want me to stay? Or call somebody? Edward?"

"No." Her voice was bleak. "I'm used to coping alone."

"Okay, then, I'll be at the Saxon in a few minutes. Lock the door behind me and call if you need anything."

I went out in the hall, waited until I heard the dead bolt slide home, and made my way to the elevator.

Great Russell Street was creepy as hell at one a.m., but I didn't realize it until I was halfway between hotels. My new heels were killing me, but my thoughts were on Abby Russell and what I was going to do if she decided to quit investigating her former friends. Now that I knew her better, little as that was, spying on her wasn't an option. If Mrs. Russell said it was over, it would have to be over, despite daughter Sunni's wishes.

The problem with me was this: I'd always hated not knowing the ending to any story. Even after I quit being a journalist and moved to Florida. Even after I traded photography and most of my intellectual curiosity for marriage and a teaching job.

That need to know only intensified after my ex-husband killed himself driving drunk and I spent two years hiding out in a friend's beach cottage. Those days are mostly a blur now — kind of like driving across Nebraska or Kansas for a really long time — but they were the most painful years of my life. To stay sane, I read boxes of books. Not biographies or histories or anything real, and not self-help or romances, which were beyond me at that point. The only safe books were mysteries, and I read them 24/7, like a smoker lighting a fresh cigarette off the butt of the last one. Everything from Conan Doyle and Rex Stout and M.C. Beaton to writers so lame they barely made paperback. By the time I left the beach, I knew who did it by Chapter 2, even in Agatha Christie's early stuff. A counselor once suggested I'd replaced my attachment to practicing alcoholics with a dangerous puzzle habit. I ignored him. My book bill was significantly cheaper than his fees and provided more comfort.

The truth is, I've always been attached to outcomes. To me, Susan Miachi's death was classic English murder stuff. I wanted to know who did it almost as much as her old friend Mrs. Russell — or at least as much as she had before the scrapbook business scared her silly.

That thought brought me back to the present. I realized I was wandering alone and overdressed in the eerie silence of Bloomsbury well after midnight. Even the traffic noise from nearby Tottenham Court Road was subdued. There was nobody else on the sidewalk. Yet, there was a sense of people everywhere, people whispering and shuffling, waiting just out of sight. Old seventeenth century ghosts or modern druggies? And waiting for what prey?

A taxi was an excellent idea but none were about. I tried to shake off my spooked feelings. Central London was supposedly awash in CCTV cameras. With Big Brother all around, how scared could you be? I ignored what might have been a footstep behind me and forced myself to walk slowly. Seconds later somebody spoke just over my shoulder, and I nearly screamed the place down.

"Sorry," Reid's stepped back, a contrite look warring with a smile. "Didn't mean to frighten you."

"What the hell are you doing here?" I was so relieved, I felt weak, and my right knee threatened to crumple beneath me.

"Waiting for you. Nigel said you were staying a few blocks from Mrs. Russell's hotel, and it occurred to me you'd walk home. Not a great place to be walking at night."

"Safer than Shoreditch or Bethnal Green," I protested.

"Maybe. But when they cleaned out the drugs around King's Cross, the users moved down here. There are a couple of needle exchanges up by the library. Anyway, I nearly missed you in the lobby." He looked down at the black book under my arm. "The infamous cuttings?"

"Yeah." I was still jittery. "Where's your car?"

"A friend's dropping it home. Can't park in Central London at night. Shall we find a drink somewhere or just stand here and chat?"

I glanced doubtfully at my watch. "What's open this late?"

"Well," he looked pleased with himself, "I did just borrow a couple bottles of Nigel's plonk before I came away." He held up a paper bag I hadn't noticed, "Saint Emilion, actually. Nigel detests bad wine; he won't even serve it to the punters. We could go to your hotel and have a drink and look at the book. I'll be happy to help you with the hard words. Or translate from English to American."

"Funny." I started to say "some other time," but I wasn't sleepy and a glass of wine and a browse among the clippings wasn't a bad idea. Maybe reading the newspaper articles would trigger additional information from Reid, something I could use to keep Abby Russell interested in Susan Miachi.

"Okay," I said, "but my hotel room doesn't run to corkscrews."

"No problem." He gave me a once-a-rocker, always-a-rocker-smile that warmed me right down to my socks. "There's one in the bag."

Chapter 15

I didn't have a suite like Mrs. Russell, but I did have chairs, a coffee table and thick bathroom glasses. I kicked off my new four inch heels, and Reid and I sat side by side and looked at the scrapbook. The Saint Emilion was exceptionally smooth; after a while my feet stopped aching.

Eventually I leaned back in my armchair and left the clippings to Reid. He either read slower than I did or he took more care. I looked at his bent head, hair curling down behind his ears and wondered if he intended to spend the night and how long it would take to get rid of him if I really wanted him to go.

I tend to be cautious about casual sex, mostly because you always pay for easy things one way or another. Also, I was involved — to a degree I didn't understand — with Tom Roddler. That thought was such an exercise in futility I almost laughed.

Here was a good looking, sexy man four feet from my bed at dark o'clock in the morning, and I was worrying about Tom. I hadn't heard from him for a week, and wherever he was and whatever he was doing, it almost certainly involved Sunni Russell.

Reid flipped back to the front of the scrapbook and studied one of the clippings. "A man called the police from the tube station?" He muttered. "Nigel never mentioned that."

"Maybe he forgot. They don't say if the voice was English or American." I rested my feet on the edge of the coffee table. "I don't suppose your dad ever kept scrapbooks?"

"I doubt it." His voice was dry. "I'd never heard of Susan Miachi or Abby Russell until a few years ago. My father and Nigel fell out back then, seriously fell out. Nigel took me to the pub for drinks and dumped the lot on me. He thought Josef was mismanaging the gallery and getting worse as he got older. He said he didn't want to dredge up the past, and then he dredged up everything he could remember all the way back to 1966. He adored Susan and he blamed Abby for her death — and Josef too."

"Does Nigel have money in the gallery?"

"If so, it's news to me. It was probably just the scotch talking because he shifted his anger to Beijing fairly quickly. Said she was dressing like Abby used to and playing Josef for a fool, and the whole time she was bonking the gallery help, particularly the gofer, Dmitri."

"Really? Are she and Dmitri an item?"

"I doubt it. She's ten years older, and he's still got spots. Just Nigel being spiteful, I expect. Anyway, I don't know where she'd find the time."

"Did you discuss the situation with your dad?"

"We don't discuss. He lectures. I listen or not, depending on the day and mood."

"But you don't think he killed Susan?"

"No." He closed the scrapbook. "No matter what the provocation, and there wasn't any so far as I know. According to Nigel and Edward, everybody liked her. Make it Abby, and you'd have suspects all over the shop."

"But what if the baby Susan was carrying was Josef's? Liz, the ex, seemed to think they were hot and heavy."

"I doubt it. Nigel never thought so, and Nigel suspects everyone of everything. Anyway, Liz is a bit paranoid. You must know that, having spoken to her."

"How do you know I spoke to her?"

He cocked an eyebrow at me. "From Edward."

"And you're sure Nigel didn't . . . ?"

"He wasn't even in the U.K. at the time. According to Edward, the police cleared him."

"Do you always discuss everything with Edward?"

"No, but he's the most detached of the three." He reached for the wine and divided the rest between our glasses. "Sometimes I think ditching the gallery and everybody's ancient, depressing baggage is the only answer. Start over somewhere warm — like Florida, perhaps. That's what we in the empire have always done." He slouched back in his chair and gave me a smart-ass smile. "Relocate to the colonies where there's no history except the kind you make yourself. How do you come to have an entire houseful of artists?"

Two glasses of red wine on an empty stomach had not only given me a buzz, it had reduced my muscles to rag doll status. I covered a yawn and slipped deeper into my chair. "The short version? I inherited a ten room house, moved in after I got flooded out of a cottage that suited me much better, and rented one room to a student who needed a quiet place to write a cookbook. She was spooked by the size of the place, and the next thing I knew she'd moved in a bunch of art grant recipients. Most of them are still there, doing whatever they do, and I play referee when necessary, teach a couple of classes at the college and surf. Bear, one of the guys in the house, taught me last year.

"What kind of artist is Bear?"

"He's a writer — Hemingway type. There's also Kenji, an Ikebana expert, who does these great underwater computer displays, and a sculptor named Jesse."

"No women?"

"Oh, sure. Nita embroiders huge panels of Florida history — don't imagine the kind your grandmother used to make — and Amy, the girl I originally rented to, has published a cookbook." I glanced sideways at him. "It's a very flexible population, and we usually have an empty room or two. Once we had a fake female playwright, a nude hairdresser, and last year a state representative's daughter with no artistic leanings at all. None of them worked out."

"Maybe you should rent me one of the empty rooms for a couple of months. The gallery couldn't possibly be slower, and it's a good time for a holiday. Unless, of course, Mrs. Russell turns out to be a problem, and I have to stick around to supervise."

"Is that why you really came to the Abbott tonight? To talk to her?"

"No, I came to see that you got home unmolested." He eyed me across his glass. "And here you are — home and unmolested."

I downed the rest of my wine and hoped I wasn't about to make a bad decision. Younger men have never been my thing.

Reid reached down and picked up one of my new heels. "Don't these hurt feet that are accustomed to walking in sand."

"Yes."

He put the shoe back on the floor, pulled my legs off the coffee table into his lap and started kneading the soles of my feet. I sighed and let him, trying not to moan out loud. Maybe he'd minored in massage at the Wharton School.

After a blissful five minutes, he said, "Are you tied up with anyone in particular at the moment?" His fingers had moved to the back of my legs, rubbing and warming the skin from ankle to knee. "The writer named Bear or anyone else?"

"Why?"

"Because I think you might be the kind of woman who can only do one thing at a time, and if so," he stopped kneading, "I'd want your full attention."

My cell phone started ringing around nine-thirty the next morning. I slid out of bed, snagged my purse off the dresser, and turned it upside down. It was probably Sunni wanting an update.

"Keegan? Can you meet me for breakfast at the Wolseley? It's newish, but Edward says it's good. We need to talk."

Not Sunni after all, Sunni's mum. "How soon?"

"Well, an hour? Is that all right?"

I looked over at Reid, sprawled against our piled-up pillows, hands clasped behind his head. He looked back with a smile I had ceased to regard as arrogant several hours earlier. At the moment, I had no desire to go anywhere. All that smooth, warm skin . . .

"Uh, sure," I said. "Where's the Wolseley?"

"Oh, right. One-sixty Piccadilly Circus. Take a cab, I'll pay for it."

I closed the cell and put it down.

"Abby Russell," I told Reid. "She wants me to meet her for

breakfast." I moved to my open suitcase and started pulling out clothes — khakis, a sweater, bra, bikinis.

"Too bad." He yawned and rubbed the back of his head. "I was going to take you to a place I know in Soho. What about tomorrow then?"

My confidence level was at least an eight this morning, and I grinned at him as I stood there naked. Who cared if the room was bright with sunlight, the kind that shows every wrinkle and blemish and pore? Who cared if his usual dates were twenty-four? "Sure, breakfast is good. Where shall we meet?"

"Oh, here, I think. I'll come by tonight, if it suits you. Make sure we're not late. In the meantime, bring that sweater and your other bits over here, and I'll show you something."

I shook my head. "Mrs. Russell's my boss, you know. At least I think she still is. I'd better get in the shower."

"If you come over here first, I'll let you be on top."

I went.

The Wolseley had originally been a luxury car showroom next to the Ritz Hotel. The cabbie ran through its entire history on the way there and assured me it was the closest thing to a Viennese coffee house that London had. He was right; the Wolseley was elegant outside and in. Very art deco with black marble pillars, vaulted ceilings, huge wrought iron chandeliers, a brass lined bar and brass reading lamps.

I was running half an hour late, but Abby Russell was still there, sitting in a black leather booth on the main floor with a cup of coffee and a basket of untouched croissants. She looked as if she'd spent the night crying, and her gold-red hair was probably as messy as it ever got. She gave me a brief good morning followed by long silence as a girl took my order for tea and laid a brown paper place mat and heavy silver cutlery in front of me.

After a moment she said, "I spoke to Steven last night. And I'm afraid it's a lost cause."

"Steven said it was a lost cause?"

"No," she admitted, "he said it was up to me to move things along, to get past the blocks. But I can't. I don't know how."

A waiter in gray pants and a black jacket brought me a silver tea pot, milk jug and a fancy tea strainer. Then he took my order for a full English breakfast and bowed himself away.

What a great place.

I gazed into a tall, ornate mirror a few feet from our table and smiled at my reflection. The forty-ish woman who smiled back at me looked barely thirty today. Her eyes were sparkling, her blonde hair fell in a shining curve, and her skin glowed. It could just have been the mirror's smoky tint, but I didn't think so. I'm way past pretending sex isn't good for your complexion.

Abby Russell was also reflected in the mirror, but she was smaller and paler and not so substantial. When I blinked she disappeared for a second, then re-formed slowly and hazily. I closed my eyes, and it happened again: the woman who almost wasn't there.

I quit blinking before the other patrons decided I was certifiable. "Did Steven say what you should do to get to the truth?"

"He said I already knew the answer. He said if you're somewhere you don't belong and you don't take yourself out, you'll be taken out."

Good old Steven. Always ready with the pithy response.

I poured milk in my cup, topped it with strong hot tea from the silver pot and took a careful swallow. It was not only delicious, it had healing properties. It warmed you all the way down, gave you hope, made you believe in God. What a fabulous day; it was at least 70 degrees outside, puffy white clouds, blue sky, glorious sun. And here was I, in the best city in the world, surrounded by elegance, eating food I didn't have to pay for. "It don't get no better than that," as somebody famous once said. If Abby Russell wanted to be exhausted and depressed, so be it, but I wasn't relinquishing my hold on ecstasy.

I devoured eggs, bacon, sausage, tomatoes, mushrooms, toast and marmalade when they arrived, but skipped the black pudding. Black pudding gives me the creeps. As I stuffed myself, Abby Russell dismembered a croissant, but she never actually got a bite all the way to her mouth.

"I could go down to Sussex and talk to Liz again," I offered finally, pushing my plate away, feeling mildly guilty.

"It wouldn't help." Mrs. Russell was rummaging in her handbag. "I thought — it wasn't supposed to . . . I thought somebody — one of them — that it was some kind of mistake. I don't think I slept twenty minutes last night. I'm going back tomorrow. I've written you a check, and I appreciate the effort you've made, but it can't be solved, any of it. We'll never know who killed Susan Miachi."

I sat, cup in hand, watching her reflection in the mirror as she talked. I was about to be fired and would, therefore, never find out who-dun-it, but only thirty percent of my brain cared. The other seventy percent was back at the hotel with Reid, remembering the warmth of his hands — and other stuff.

A woman's loud voice, at a table behind us, sliced through my libidinous thoughts. The voice was loud and caustic. "It was her first flight anywhere! Can you imagine in this day and age — not flying until you were fifty-two?"

Those first six words triggered my freaky auditory memory and bits and pieces of stored away conversation began to filter into my head. I now heard, suddenly and clearly, Abby

Russell on our flight over, boozed up and confiding: "It was my first flight anywhere. We landed in Halifax and Reykjavik and Luxembourg with engine trouble."

And that stirred memories of other conversations.

Abby reminiscing at Rule's: "Where I grew up, there were only two kinds of sin, and venial didn't count."

Nigel at the Tate Modern in his elegant cream suit: "Her parents were free Presbyterian or some off brand."

Edward showing his photo of the four of them in front of Big Ben: "Abby was younger actually by nearly a year; we celebrated her birthday the week before Susan died.

And finally, Sunni Russell at the beach: "Mom's an Aries. Always falls on her feet."

"Did you hear me?" Abby Russell made no attempt to keep the impatience out of her voice. "It isn't possible. Nobody will ever find out who killed her."

Very carefully I set my cup back in its saucer, remembering the Tiroler Hut and the devastated look on her face when she realized Nigel was gay and always had been.

"You're right, they won't," I said and eyed her with something close to admiration, "because Susan Miachi isn't dead. She's been calling herself Abby Russell for forty-seven years."

Chapter 16

In the seconds that followed, our table floated silently in the Wolseley's sea of civilized clamor. Patrons laughed and chattered, regulars called to each other from the two narrow balconies at the back of the room, and the woman at the next table tapped her knife as she emphasized the numerous ways Rhodes was superior to Crete.

Abby Russell sat very still, check in upraised hand. Finally she murmured,

"What on earth are you saying?"

"I'm remembering what you said on the plane. You landed in Halifax and Reykjavík and Luxembourg on your first flight anywhere. Those were your words. That means you were working your way across the Atlantic toward England, not coming from it. You also said you grew up with venial sin. Abby Pell wouldn't have, she wasn't Catholic; but Susan Miachi probably was. And your daughter Sunni told me you were an Aries. That puts your birthday in March or April. Edward said the four of you celebrated Abby Pell's birthday just before Susan was killed — in November."

Her eyes slid away from me; the lines around her mouth sharpened. "I don't know what I said on the plane. I must have mixed it all up or you misunderstood."

I shook my head and ticked off points on my fingers. "You were both redheads and the dead girl's face was battered for starters. Even in Edward's photographs I couldn't tell the two of you apart. You're a totally different girl from the Abby your friends describe, and you've talked willingly to everybody except Josef. Why? Because he was the one person who'd know absolutely you weren't her." I paused as the realization hit me. "Except Liz knew, didn't she? That's why you left her cottage in such a hurry. She knew you were Susan as soon as she saw you."

"You can't — those little things don't mean anything. You've mixed it all up. Abby was identified, recognized. Her face — it was some terrible, horrible mistake . . ."

"No. Whoever did it knew exactly who she was, kept hitting her for that very reason. Everybody liked Susan, but they resented hell out of Abby."

The second I said it out loud, I knew it was the absolute truth.

She placed the signed check on the table and put her hands in her lap. "I think you've let Susan's story get away from you." She spaced the words out carefully. "Susan's dead, Keegan. She's been dead longer than you've been alive."

"I don't think so. Your memories of Nigel were all good ones, loving ones even, but he and Abby hated each other, were barely speaking at the end. And you were honestly shocked that

Nigel was gay, something Abby would have known all along. Susan was a little naive, more concerned with kindness than uncomfortable truth. That's what Steven told you on the phone, isn't it? Not to find the truth, but to tell it to get things moving? He said you were the block."

"I hope you're not going to mention these wild ideas to my daughter." Her voice had retreated about six thousand miles and those green eyes were cool; strictly the Abby Russell with big bucks who wielded clout when necessary.

I shook my head. "It's your story, you can tell her what you want her to know. I was only hired to find her father. Which I haven't. About all I can do is refund her money and get on the next plane home." Well, maybe not the *next* plane, I amended silently, thinking of Reid.

She looked instantly relieved. "You won't lose out. This is still yours." She pushed the check across the table to me.

"No." I didn't want to be bought off. I said it quickly before the amount registered with me. Five thousand dollars. Shit, five thousand bought a lot of air conditioning. Even for a house filled with energy-sucking artists.

"But you have to, otherwise . . ." she broke off, brows drawn together. "Sunni won't come over here, will she? I don't want Edward or any of them bothered. It's best she doesn't even get a hint —"

"If they didn't tell us anything useful, why would they tell her?"

"I don't know. She has ways — she's very persuasive." She rubbed at the corners of her eyes with twitching fingers. "I wish to God I'd never started this. It just goes on and on. You can't get out."

"Then end it." I said impatiently. "Didn't Steven say you'd get an opportunity to make things right, even if it was out of character or really hard? That if you missed that opportunity, it would be gone forever? Maybe this is your shot. Otherwise, you're back where you started, nightmares and all."

"You can't go back . . . not once you . . ." She put both elbows on the table and leaned her face into open palms. "I am Abby Russell." Her voice was emphatic. "I'm the girl who moved to California and lived in a commune. I'm the housewife who —"

There was a lot more, some of it to do with raising children and charity donations and nursing a sick husband, but I lost her after the first sentence because I was mentally banging my head on the table. I squeezed my eyes shut and made a face. How could I be so thick?

"What's wrong?" Mrs. Russell had stopped muttering. "Why are you looking that way?"

"Rampant stupidity attack." I waved a hand. "Your husband gave Sunni a picture of the three of you taken at the commune when she was a baby. All I had to do was show it to Edward, or any of them, and ask who the girl was. But I tucked it away and forgot all about it."

This time her poker face failed her. You could almost see the thoughts flickering in her green eyes: "There were no pictures. He wouldn't do that. How good a likeness was it? Why did he keep it all those years without saying anything? Why give it to Sunni and not tell me?

"A picture." She repeated the two words as if the water was up to her neck and the ark was completely full.

I looked at my watch. "It's early, but I think we need a drink. I'm exhausted, for reasons we don't need to go into, and you're exhausted because Abby Russell — Abby Pell — has been dead forever and you don't know what to do about it." I grinned at her. "So I'm buying, and if you want, if it makes you feel any better at all, you can tell me the story over a scotch and water, and it goes no farther. I'm your guardian angel, right? The right initials — K. S.? You don't have to pay guardian angels to keep quiet."

She sat, staring at the wall and not a muscle moved. The longer she stared, the more red-rimmed her eyes became. I didn't see any tears, but there must have been some because she wiped her eyes and smeared whatever she'd used to cover the dark circles.

"Sorry," she said, rubbing some more and increasing the raccoon look. "Confiding in people isn't my strength. No practice." The last word dissolved to a whisper.

I handed her the napkin off my lap, the part that wasn't smeared with marmalade. "You don't have to confide anything, it was just a suggestion. I'll give you the picture or burn it if you'd rather. But I'm having a drink anyway." I turned to look for the waiter.

"Yes, me too. Better make mine a double."

When I looked surprised she managed a weak smile. "I know when I'm licked. Steven said this would happen, but I . . . he's never wrong." She sucked in a breath and reached for her cell phone. "I'd like Edward to hear too. I may not be able to tell it once, let alone twice."

Edward was apparently on her speed dial because she pushed only one button and spoke almost immediately.

"It's Ab — it's me," she told him. "Could you possibly meet Keegan and me at the Wolseley? Right away? No, I'm fine, I just need to talk to you, if you could manage . . . " She closed the phone and dropped it in her purse. "He's on another call, but he's coming." She stood up and smoothed down her blue suede jacket. "I'll go clean up while you order."

I nodded, but I was betting even money, she'd disappear the minute she was out of sight.

My own poker face must not have been working because one corner of her mouth twisted and she shook her head. "I won't do a runner, Keegan, I promise. It's only, well, it's Edward. I can't imagine how he's going to take this."

I stared back at her, amazed. "I can't imagine how he's going to explain identifying you as Abby in 1966."

"You never really looked alike — the two of you." Edward face was pale beneath his tan, and he kept fiddling with his shirt sleeves, rolling and re-rolling them. "Not really. It was the red hair — and the green sweatshirt. And Abby was away, we thought." He frowned at the untouched scotch and soda in front of him. "Too much like going down a horrible memory lane. Big white D, blood everywhere, face mashed about. I only looked for a second, but it never occurred to me . . . and then the newspapers got onto the Mafia husband." He stopped, straightened and said, "What on earth were you thinking? Why didn't you tell someone?"

Sunni's mother, at least I assumed she was really Sunni's mother, had freshened her makeup, smoothed her hair and was halfway through a second drink. She looked considerably more alive than she had twenty minutes earlier and a great deal calmer. Maybe she'd popped a couple of anti-anxiety caps in the ladies' room.

She had done the thing right, meeting Edward at the entrance and walking him up and down the sidewalk as she explained who she wasn't. I got only a glimpse of them as they passed the front entrance, disappeared, then passed it again half a minute later. The explanation took so long that I decided Edward wasn't coming in and maybe Abby, I mean Susan, wasn't either. She had taken her purse with her, and I started counting up my cash in case I got stuck with the breakfast tab, as well as two scotches. I'd just decided I was two pounds and a tip short when in they came.

Edward threw himself into a chair without saying hello, voiced his first reaction and repeated: "What on earth were you thinking? Why didn't you tell someone?"

Susan drew in a breath. "I thought Tony sent someone after me and Abby got in the way. I just cowered there — beside her — for the longest time, and then I realized somebody was in the flat. Hiding, making scrabbling noises." She shuddered. "Like an animal."

The same kind you thought you heard at your hotel door, I thought.

It took Edward a second to realize how stunned he was. "You were actually there? You saw her dead?"

She nodded. "I lied about going to Stratford that day. Abby talked me into Coventry instead — laying a false trail, she called it — so she could be alone with Josef. But the whole trip was a disaster. I was sick to my stomach that morning, and it poured down rain and the hotel room was so depressing, I just turned around and came back to town. Josef was supposed to leave for Brussels, but he was really going straight to the flat when the gallery closed. I hadn't taken my painting gear, and I thought I could beat him home and get it and go to the Y for a couple of nights. I'd have gone crazy sitting around doing nothing.

"But the front door wasn't locked and the hall light was out and Abby was sprawled on the lounge floor. It was just so unreal. When I heard somebody moving around, I panicked and grabbed her backpack by mistake. Later I found her passport in it and quite a chunk of money."

Edward frowned at her. "Why didn't you call the police?"

"I don't know, all I could think of was getting away. Maybe

if I'd seen a policeman . . ." She rubbed the back of her hands as if they were cold. "I thought of going upstairs to you, but I was scared, and I just kept running. When I got to the Y, I was horribly sick again, and then I fell asleep. Some girl woke me up, banging on the door and screaming they'd given me her room by mistake. I was so out of it I didn't even ask for another room, just carried my stuff to the top of the road. That was surreal too. All those placards at the newspaper kiosk, big black-scrawled letters, jumping out at me about an American girl murdered in Earls Court. I knew it wouldn't be long before Tony found out it was really Abby, and they'd be after me. So I took the boat train from Victoria. When I got to France, I used Abby's passport in case anyone was looking for me, but customs waved me through without paying any real attention. Passport pictures were black and white back then, and we had the same hair and general description. Besides, there were no terrorists in those days; I was just another hippie kid backpacking around Europe."

"They didn't check it in Greece?" Edward picked up his drink and downed about half of it.

"Another lie. I never went to Greece." Her grin was lopsided, but she made the effort. "On the train to Paris I thought about Australia or some other place Tony wouldn't look, but I was too scared. In the end I got on a plane to New York. An American girl I met in Soho had once lived at a commune near San Francisco. She said they'd take anybody in, and she was right. I tried to sound English and told myself I was really Abby and Susan was just somebody I used to know. Gerry was already there, totally messed up on drugs, and we got close. By the time we married, I was Abby Pell to everybody, and I used her passport for the marriage application. Gerry was so in and out those days, he never questioned anything; I felt safe keeping my own birthday. It was the only thing left that was really mine."

"But you were still legally married to Tony," I said, "when you married Gerry?"

"True. Or so I thought. He'd been dead a couple of months by then," her chin went up, "but I didn't know it. Or care. My family was all gone, and I was never going back. Once Gerry got better, he was a wonderful husband and didn't mind if I was a little bit of a hermit. When we took a driving trip to Mexico, I applied for a new passport with Abby's old one. A friend of Gerry's hurried it through and afterward I put Susan Miachi in mothballs. The past just — wasn't anymore. No more Tony or his creepy friend Earl, no dead girl in a basement flat. But after Gerry died the nightmares started. Steven said neither Tony nor Earl killed Abby, so I hired a detective to check. Tony had died after falling down some stairs a few months after he got out of jail. And somebody shot Earl shortly after I left Rhode Island."

I took a sip of my warm, straight up, Famous Grouse. "So you'd been Tony-free all those years and didn't know it?"

She nodded. "It was a huge relief, that and knowing I hadn't caused Abby's death. But Steven said London was unfinished business and if I could deal with it in person, I could chase my old demons away . . . all of them." She looked across the table at Edward. "So, I had the detectives find out where you all were, and I came back."

Edward's color was improving, booze for breakfast will do that, but his frown seemed permanently embedded. "I understand about finding her," he said, "but the dead girl was pregnant, Abby had an abortion."

"She didn't. Another lie. Liz couldn't have children and Abby wanted the baby. She was going to tell Josef that weekend."

"So," Edward's forehead began to smooth a little as he

worked it out, "so, there's no reason you can't be who you really are now — Susan Miachi?"

"Susan Russell," she corrected. "whoever that is. I went from Susan Johnson to Susan Miachi to Abby Russell to now. Your guess is as good as mine."

They exchanged a fairly intense look before she turned to me. "Well, Keegan, now what?"

"I guess it's up to you and your buddy Steven. Is telling your story enough to lose the demons? Or should we find out who left the scrapbook?'

"What scrapbook?" Edward's frown was back and Abby/Susan's explanation about the cuttings left at her hotel didn't do much to alleviate it. He groaned and ordered another round of drinks. "God, it never ends."

She nodded in agreement, still looking at him but talking to both of us. "Can't we just make it end? I don't want to talk to everybody again. What happened was tragic enough. And nobody knows but the three of us."

"And whoever killed her," I said.

Silence. Then she straightened her shoulders and lifted her chin. "We couldn't prove it even if we found out, but if you think I'm copping out again — just because I'm feeling this incredible sense of relief — say so. If you don't, I vote to let it go."

Edward obviously agreed. After only a second's hesitation, he picked up his scotch, tapped it against her glass as it sat on the table and drained it.

She took an answering sip of hers, and they sat grinning at each other as if they were forty years younger and no one they knew had ever died.

I swallowed the slight trace of disappointment I felt. "Then you'll tell Sunni about her father and the other things she needs to know?" I said to Susan.

"Yes." She dragged her eyes away from Edward for a second. "I — we're definitely due for a talk."

I nodded and lifted my glass to both of them. "To sleeping dogs, then."

Chapter 17

When I left the Wolseley, Edward was ordering coffee and sandwiches, and Abby/Susan was wolfing down croissants. They seemed almost giddy with relief and insisted I join them for dinner that evening. When I said I had a date they insisted on the following night. Then they forgot all about me.

Outside the air was crisp and cool with a steadily warming sun. I threaded my way through bands of tourists headed in the direction of Buckingham Palace. From the conversations they seemed to be mostly English, up from the country for a vacation in the capitol. Good choice, considering the economy. I headed east on Piccadilly and Shaftsbury toward Charing Cross Road, and the longer I walked, the more relieved I felt.

Mrs. Russell could deal with the problem of Sunni's father and her own identity concerns. My job — jobs — were over. Susan Miachi wasn't dead, Abby Pell was, and that murder would probably never be solved. I had a full week left in London to do exactly as I pleased, and the first thing I intended to do was go back to bed.

I had just turned north on Charing Cross Road when my cell phone started jangling. Since I'd just left Mrs. Russell, didn't want to talk to Tom Roddler, and had nothing to report to Sunni, I ignored it. Nobody else had my number, and I was sorry now I'd given it to Tom.

The ringing, however, didn't stop. When it began to come at three minute intervals, I started thinking emergency and detoured into the park at Leicester Square. I pulled the phone out of my shoulder bag and muttered a tentative hello.

"How's London?" said Sunni Russell's uber-cheerful voice. "It's hot as hell here. I got your message. Sorry I'm late calling back, I've been kind of, uh, tied up."

Tied up? Is Tom into bondage these days? I banished that visual as I considered and discarded several possible answers to her question.

"Well," I said finally, "your mother's decided to stop looking into her friend Susan Miachi's death."

"Really? She just started. What about family members? Has she met up with anybody at all?"

"Just the people I told you about at the gallery — from the Sixties."

"Right, Edward and Nigel and Josef, right? Does she seem closer to one of them than to the others? They're in the right age frame, right? For my father?"

I hesitated longer than I intended. "It's hard to say. I just met her for breakfast. She's going to talk to you — today or tomorrow, I expect."

Silence.

Finally, "What is it you're not telling me, Keegan? You're working for me, remember? Me first. Not my mother."

"True, but I haven't found out what you want to know, and I don't see that changing. I'll be happy to refund part of your money —"

"Whoa! Hold on. Are you quitting on me? Is she paying you more? Is that it?"

"No." I was suddenly happier about declining the $5,000 check. "She's not paying me at all. I just think you'd better rely on your mother for what you want to know."

"Oh, sure. She's never told me a single thing she didn't have to in my entire life."

"Well, she's — she's looking in some new directions, you know how things change." It sounded lame, and I knew it. "She said she'd talk to you, and it's her story to tell, Sunni, not mine."

It was so quiet on the other end I thought she'd hung up on me. I got up, walked around a small flock of pigeons and drifted up Charing Cross Road. "Hello? You still there?"

"Yeah." Her voice was subdued. "Shit. I could call her, I guess. Listen, don't give up on me yet. Just stay put while I think this through, okay? It's hard to make decisions when you're so far away. I'll call you tomorrow. Can you just sit tight 'til tomorrow?"

I said I could and disconnected with relief. By tomorrow she and her mother should have worked it out. I turned the phone off so I didn't get caught again before I reached the hotel.

Reid was long gone but the sheets still smelled like him. For once I appreciated the Saxon's less than speedy room service. I put the Do Not Disturb sign on my doorknob, stretched out on the unmade bed and closed my eyes.

Twenty minutes later, I was still wide awake. The problem was the newspaper clippings. My mind wouldn't leave it alone, not with the answer only a couple of blocks away.

Great Russell Street was crowded with tourists doing the British Museum. I passed Karl's Café, where I'd first kept watch on Mrs. Russell's hotel, crossed the street and entered the glass doors of the Abbott Hotel. Abby/Susan and Edward could decide what they liked; I wanted to know about the damned scrapbook.

There were only two people at the hotel's front desk, an Indian girl hovering over a computer and a pale man with very little hair and fewer people skills. The man admitted being on duty the night before but refused to say if he remembered a package for Mrs. Russell, even when I waved a ten pound note at him. He said if Mrs. Russell had questions or concerns about the delivery, he would be happy to discuss it with her, emphasis on *her*. He was right, of course, but I deal poorly with officiousness when I'm short on sleep. I turned away before he finished explaining his position. Bribery always worked in the movies. What was his problem?

Just as I reached the lobby's front doors, someone called "Madam, madam," and the Indian girl caught up with me.

We were around the corner and out of sight of the front desk, but she kept her voice down anyway. "I'm very sorry, madam, Marki doesn't . . ." She paused and started over: "I also was on duty last night, and it was a woman who left the package. In a plakkie bag — a supermarket bag. She was blonde, but the hair was a wig. I noticed right away."

"A wig?" I remembered the woman who followed me around my first day in town. "Was she thin, long blond hair, very high heels?"

"Oh, no," the girl said in a soft voice, "quite old, in a raincoat. Her eyes only opened part way when she spoke."

I thanked her, gave her the ten pound note and told her not to share with Marki. Unless Nigel had taken to walking around in drag, I was pretty sure who'd been scrapbooking in her spare time. Good old Liz.

I decided to call Abby/Susan as I headed back to my hotel. Not to tell her about the clippings, since she and Edward had voted against, but to warn her that Sunni had phoned.

Our connection began with static and dead spaces and only got worse. When a giggling voice said, "Hello" for the third time, I thought I'd punched up a teeny bopper by mistake. But, no, it was only the newly discovered Susan Russell.

"Keegan? We're just leaving the restaurant. Edward has an appointment. He's getting me a cab. You have no idea how much I appreciate what you did — what we did — today. I feel like I've shed this eighty pound winter coat I've been wearing forever. I feel so light, so free. Sorry, sorry, I'm rattling on. Did you want me for something?"

"Just giving you a heads up. Your daughter called, and I referred her to you. She thinks I've sold her out; it's possible she'll catch the next flight over and insist on knowing everything. I'm sorry."

"It's okay, don't worry about it. Edward and I talked it over, and I have a plan. I'll phone Steven and make sure it's okay, but I think it's probably best." Her voice fragmented away as screeching, tearing sounds and more static took its place. This was followed by a hollow thump and faint buzzing.

"Abb — Susan? Are you there?"

No answer. "Susan? Susan!"

In a less than brilliant move, I shook the phone. The buzzing stopped. I shook it again and got no sound at all. Our connection, however tenuous, was gone.

My taxi driver was speedy and he knew a lot of tricks, but several thousand people had paid the 8-pound-Congestion-Charge for the privilege of clogging up Central London, and they were all getting their money's worth. By the time we reached the Wolseley neither Edward nor Susan was in sight. One of the doormen at the nearby Ritz informed me that an American woman had popped right off the sidewalk into the traffic near some scaffolding; she seemed to be badly hurt, and he didn't know where the ambulance had taken her. I kept dialing her cell phone number, but it was either turned off, broken or being ignored.

There was a chance the woman wasn't her, but I knew in my heart it was. I had no way to reach Edward. Reid would have to do.

I fished Reid's card out of my purse and called the gallery. It was a long time before he came to the phone, and then he sounded distracted and short of breath. He told me they were moving heavy sculptures for an exhibit, gave me Edward's number without asking why I wanted it and said he'd see me around eight.

Edward's mobile phone rang a dozen plus times, but I hung on for lack of a better idea. On the fifteenth ring, he answered. Mrs. Russell had been injured in a traffic accident, and she was at St. Mary's Hospital near Paddington Station. I was already in another taxi and on the way before I remembered the tube was faster.

When I got there Edward was leaning against a wall in the waiting area of the hospital's Emergency Department. He was so calm, so detached, that it was a few minutes before I realized how furious he was.

"Quite a lot of bruising," he informed me, "wrist sprained, but not shattered, they believe. She was pushed. Again." He glared at a wall. "I only walked a little way to flag a taxi. I only left her for a second."

I nodded, eyes on his face. "Have you seen her? Will they keep her here?"

His head moved back and forth slightly. "No to both. She should be released in a couple of hours. When that happens I'm driving her to Derbyshire. I'll have to —" He broke off, then said, "I've got her hotel keys. I don't know whether —" He frowned at me. "You wouldn't like to go pack up some of her things? Enough for a few days and meet me back here? I don't want to leave her. But make sure nobody follows you from the hotel."

I hesitated, and his blue eyes narrowed. "Pack a bag for yourself as well, if you like. You probably consider me no more trustworthy than the others."

"Where in Derbyshire?"

"What?" He blinked at me. "Oh. A small farm I bought sometime back. Eight acres, four rented out to local farmers for hay. Electric lights, running water, three bedrooms, one bath. Three hours by car. I often go up there to write."

"Okay. I'll be back."

I took the tube to the Abbott, used the keys Edward had given me, and threw some of Susan's clothes and cosmetics into a suitcase. Then I carried the bag down the street to the Saxon and repeated the exercise for myself. The guy on the front desk promised to keep my room 'til I returned and got me a cab for Euston Station. On the way there I called Reid, but he'd gone to lunch. I left a message that I'd be out of town with Mrs. Russell for a couple of days and would call later.

At Euston I dragged both suitcases down into the Underground, took the Circle line two stops beyond Paddington and hauled everything out again. Then I crossed to the opposite tunnel and caught a train back. I watched all the way for blondes with shopping bags or anyone else who looked familiar. By the time Edward stowed our suitcases in the trunk — or rather boot — of his Volvo and I collapsed into his front seat, I was sure nobody had followed me, but I was too exhausted to care.

I twisted around to make sure that Susan, tucked up in Edward's back seat and apparently sedated, was still breathing. Edward seemed disinclined for conversation, which suited me fine. I intended to concentrate on any suspicious vehicles that followed us out of town. Unfortunately, I was asleep long before we reached the Ring Road and headed north. Having sex all night at twenty-four is one thing, doing it at forty-two is something else.

Chapter 18

If you drive two hours north and slightly west out of London, you run straight into Derbyshire. Edward's house was located in the pastoral part of the county, all green hills, obscure villages and small farms. It was a photographer's dream, if you were packing a wide angle lens, but I was groggy, tired and regretting my headlong flight to the country. I'm not big on weekending in the wilds anyway, and I enjoy it less with near-strangers. Edward was still an unknown quantity. If he turned out to be the bad guy, what the hell was I going to do about it? When he stopped for milk and a loaf of bread at a small village a mile from the farmhouse, I almost bailed and went looking for the nearest train.

The farmhouse was a two story gray stone structure with a kitchen garden and several out buildings. After bringing in the luggage, Edward and I helped Susan, still dazed and obviously in pain, from the car to the living room, which he called the lounge. The lounge was bone-chillingly cold with flagstone floors and musty carpeting. Edward collected half a dozen small logs out back and built a fire in the fireplace before going to the kitchen to make tea. I helped Susan (Would I ever get used to calling her that?) settle her banged-up self on a worn, tweed sofa, covered her with a maroon afghan and followed Edward into the kitchen.

The kitchen was painted soft butter yellow and had casement windows that looked over an orchard. Edward filled a kettle and put it on to boil before opening the windows wide. Sunlight drifted gently in, and a breeze that smelled of apple and cherry trees moved the thin white curtains back and forth. The breeze was warmer than the inside of the house.

I had at least a dozen pertinent remarks ready, but I lacked the energy to make them. Instead I sat and studied something I'd never seen in a kitchen before: a collection of old and extremely dusty cameras on a shelf over the stove. There were probably twenty or more up there, all jumbled together.

When the kettle boiled, Edward rinsed the teapot to warm it, shoveled in a tablespoon of loose tea, added scalding water and popped a flowered tea cosy over the top. Almost as good as the Wolseley, I thought wistfully, but it seemed days, not hours, since the three of us had breakfasted there.

"Five minutes." His voice was thin in the silence. "Would you mind digging up some garlic from the garden? I'll need it for spaghetti sauce. That corner there." He pointed out the window at a section of stone wall. "Trowel on a hook by the back door."

I found the trowel, went out to the wall and dug around until I located six or seven small white bulbs. Back in the kitchen I washed and trimmed them with a paring knife while Edward laid the table with a cloth, blue cups and plates and a tub of Irish butter.

Susan insisted on having her tea in the kitchen, although it took a while to get her there. She moved slowly, each step accompanied by an obvious spasm of pain. From the look of the bruises, road rash and swelling around her neck and arms, she would hurt more tomorrow. Her arm was packed in an ice bandage and rested in a sling with a tiny padded pillow. She drank her tea left handed and ignored the slice of bread on her plate.

I drank three cups of tea, ate hot, thickly buttered toast, and felt surprisingly better. The yellow kitchen was cheerful, though everything in it was clean, worn and seventy years old. There was no television, no land phone I could see, and the only electric appliance was a beat up toaster. Probably boring as hell after three days, but at the moment definitely a port in a storm.

Susan said thank you, no thank you, and not much else, but when Edward poured me — and himself — a shot from an ancient bottle of Napoleon brandy, she protested being excluded.

"Two pain medications before bedtime," he reminded her.

She got a stubborn look and held out the glass until he poured her a shot too.

The brandy was even more soothing than the tea. Susan and I sipped it companionably as we watched Edward stir my hand-picked garlic into a mix of onions, green peppers and tomatoes. When the mix was simmering in a sauce pan, he took us on a tour of the kitchen garden, which was mostly red currant and raspberry bushes.

"The orchard wants a good raking," he conceded with a frown, "but I have a man who paints up periodically and mows the grass . . ."

"We were going to let it go," Susan interrupted him, her thoughts obviously not on fruit bushes, "but somebody didn't — didn't —"

"Know what you decided?" I finished for her. "Maybe some-body thinks you know more than you do."

She shook her head, said she wanted to go back inside, and fell asleep almost as soon as she reached the couch. Warmth from the fire filled the room and cast a healing glow over the bruises on her face.

In the kitchen Edward decided his spaghetti sauce was too watery and chucked in half a cup of the Napoleon Brandy.

"You don't cook with expensive stuff like that," I objected.

He grinned and sloshed in a little more. "There was quite a lot of it here when I bought the place lock, stock and barrel. Couldn't believe it. It's a sort of cure-all really — bee stings, shock, lie-detector, bad decisions. Wait 'til you see how it thickens the sauce."

He was right. By dinnertime, the Spaghetti Bolognese was perfect. He cut Susan's up in small pieces, carried it to the lounge, and hand-fed her most of it as if she were a baby. I ate with them in front of the fire and tried not to gag at their behavior.

Afterward, I carried our bowls into the kitchen, filled the sink with hot water and washing up liquid, and pushed up my sleeves. I soaped, rinsed, dried and put everything away, reveling in the silence and cool evening air. *A world away from dishwashers, air conditioning and television.*

As I wiped down the wooden table Edward had used as a work space, I tried to keep my eyes from wandering to the shelf above the stove. The cameras there were so thick with dust it looked like they were wearing fuzzy coats. Eventually I couldn't stand it, climbed on a chair, wiped each camera and cleaned the shelf. One of the cameras was a 35 mm Pentax, the same one I'd used on my last few assignments. I was still on the chair, checking its light meter when I saw Edward and Susan watching me from the doorway.

"Susan's giving up," Edward said, as he steered her toward the stairway. He eyed the Pentax in my hands. "I might have film for that somewhere if you're interested."

"Oh, no thanks, I don't do that anymore. Just checking." I put it back on the shelf like it was burning my fingers and listened to them climb the stairs to the landing. There were only fifteen narrow steps, but it took a long time.

I helped myself to more brandy, went back to the lounge and curled into a wing backed chair. It was only 8:30, and the sun was still bright outside, but we'd all had a very long day. I sat and drank and watched the fire burn itself gently away. Once I thought I could hear giggling upstairs, but it was probably just the wind.

When Edward returned he had a drink of his own, and we sat together, not talking, for a long time.

"Who is it?" I said finally. "You must have an idea who's doing this."

"You'd think so, wouldn't you? I've known them all so long." He kept his eyes on the last smoldering log. "I actually didn't recognize her, you know. I just kept thinking that a Californian lifestyle and all that money had drained the wild out of her. Or that the years had slowed her down. I liked her more than I had in the Sixties, but I should have known — should have sensed . . ."

I shrugged. "You thought you saw her body in nineteen sixty-six."

"Still. They were so totally different."

"She got through customs in two countries on Abby's passport," I reminded him, "and traded it for a new one in California. There was certainly a superficial resemblance in the pictures you gave me."

"True, the hair, the pointed chin, but Christ, I'm a photographer." He re-rolled one of the sleeves on his blue cotton shirt.

"I'm used to really looking at things. And I knew Abby wore Susan's clothes, with permission or without, if she felt like it. It just never occurred to me . . ."

I watched him over the rim of my cup. I was pretty sure he was out of it, but I've been fooled by the best, and more than once. On the other hand, he was drinking the Napoleon, the brandy he claimed was an antidote to lies.

"I'm not sure I understand about Abby," I said. "She had flings with you, Josef, practically everybody. Did she have one with Nigel too?"

"Possible, I suppose. Gender bending was a hot number back then, although he never seemed interested in anyone except Josef." An odd look passed over Edward's face. "Lord, I'd forgotten. Once, about a year after Susan died, Nigel turned up in London, and we met at a pub. He'd been down in Cornwall staying with friends, but he was a mess, maudlin, depressed, drinking too much. He got on a crying jag, and, well, it's possible he was just trying to impress me or deflect questions about his . . ."

"Go on," I said impatiently, "What did he say?"

"He said he'd never forget how cold it was that winter and how Susan and he had often slept in the same bed together for warmth, particularly when Abby came home late or didn't come home at all."

I leaned back in my chair.

So Nigel isn't out of the running after all.

Chapter 19

When I woke the next morning, the house was freezing. I stayed where I was, warm and drowsy, under a wool quilt pieced from squares of somebody's old coats and sweaters. When I woke the second time, sun was angling in through the bedroom window, and I remembered where I was — Derbyshire — and where I wasn't — London. And London reminded me that I hadn't talked to Reid, who didn't easily fit the description of a vacation fling. Vacation romances shouldn't come with strings, particularly not those attached to an old murder or attempts at a new one. What had been an exercise in puzzle solving now seemed stupid, dangerous meddling. After another ten minutes I sighed, threw off the blankets and forced myself up. There was only one bathroom in the farmhouse, and I wanted first shot at it.

The bathroom had yellow wallpaper, pink shag carpeting, a burnt orange commode and an extra long pale green bathtub. The window over the tub was open and the arctic air ruled out a leisurely soak. I washed quickly at the sink, shivered into jeans and sweater, and went to look for food.

Breakfast is my true north every time. Ply me with coffee, and I'll believe anything — like maybe Mrs. Russell was merely shaken up by her injury and would actually benefit from a stay in the country. Add some bacon and scrambled eggs, and I'd decide she'd just been careless in Piccadilly traffic. With an admission like that we could all get back to what we were doing before she screwed up.

The kitchen was clammy and cold, I couldn't find the coffee maker, and I didn't feel like waiting around until somebody got up who knew where one was. I went outside, liberated a rake from an unlocked storage shed and started scraping up twigs and leaves and dead apples from the orchard floor. Vigorously. By the time Edward opened the kitchen window and the smell of freshly brewed caffeine drifted out into the garden, parts of the orchard floor were swept clean and I wasn't cold anymore.

Mrs. Russell was up and dressed, picking at dry toast from a rack. She'd put on makeup and done something to her hair, but the left side of her face was red, purple and emerging yellow. She ignored my good morning, her mind obviously elsewhere. But after Edward slid a tomato and cheese omelet in front of me and sat down to eat one of his own, she launched into speech. And not dot-dot-dot style, either. Pain medication apparently rendered Sunni's mom crystal clear, opinionated and miffed.

"One minute I was standing there," she fumed, "and the next I'm staring down the driver of a Metrocab. But the worst thing was the voice. Not the man who kept asking if I'd broken anything or heard a popping sound. The other voice. The one that growled, 'Just die,' like a snake would if it could talk. I hate snakes."

"Did you recognize the voice?" I said. "Male or female?"

"No."A shudder went all through her. "But whoever it was hated me."

"Or hated Abby?"

"True." She pushed her untouched coffee aside. "I've been so busy dumping secrets on the two of you, I forgot the others don't know."

"Liz knew," I reminded her, "and she was probably still in London yesterday morning. She was certainly there the night before when she left the scrapbook at your hotel."

Susan and Edward opened their mouths at the same time, but Edward got in first. "How do you know that?" he demanded.

"I bribed the desk clerk at the Abbott."

The room was silent for longer than was comfortable. Edward looked like he hadn't slept much, and his thick silver hair was ruffled. Still, he was a hot number, even first thing in the morning. His blue eyes fixed on Susan as he spoke.

"I doubt Liz . . . Perhaps we should ring up everyone involved and say you're letting the matter drop. Returning to California." When she didn't answer he added, "Or you can stay here until we get visas for Africa, and we'll just go."

Africa? That was the plan? I wondered what Steven would say to that. Probably, "If you run away from your troubles, you'll carry your troubles along with you." Good old, profound Steven.

"We could." Susan shifted in her chair and winced at the pain. "Look, I don't want to make a mistake this time. I've been getting it wrong for years. Running off in a panic. I want this finished, but I don't know . . . I need some time. I'm going to have to think."

To me that meant a transatlantic call to Steven as soon as breakfast was over. I was wrong.

After a snail crawl around the rose bushes in the garden, Susan spent the next six hours on a lounge chair Edward set up for her under a tree. Most of the time she appeared to be sleeping, which probably beat hell out of thinking.

Derbyshire rolled out all of its best assets that afternoon, warm sun, cloudless skies, hazy purple hills and the pervading scent of newly mown hay. The only sounds were birds chirping in the apple trees and bees buzzing the pile of orchard bits I'd raked up earlier.

Around three in the afternoon Edward walked down to see a neighbor who raised goats and returned with cylinders of goat cheese and a jug of homemade wine. I packed my suitcase to go back to town but delayed departure until Susan decided what to do. It wasn't that she needed me for anything, not with Edward around, it just felt wrong to abandon her with everything in such a mess.

I put off calling Reid until I knew the plan, prowled the grounds for a while and ended up back in the kitchen checking out Edward's shelf of cameras. There was an old Brownie box, one of the original Polaroid Land cameras, a Leica that probably dated from the Thirties, a Rolliflex and a dozen others that had been in use before my time. You can do some interesting things with old cameras — fiddle with the light meters, smear Vaseline on the lens to create a misty look. Even a shot of the open kitchen window with that shaft of sunlight angling in across the linoleum wasn't a bad idea.

I stopped the thought in its tracks. The last time I dragged out my camera and shot a few rolls to spite my ex-husband, he ended up dead on a country road. Not that I believe, deep down, there's a correlation between photography and death.

I just don't like taking a chance.

Late in the afternoon, dark gray clouds began rolling in from the north, and rain soon followed. Edward didn't feel like cooking, so Susan and I hustled out to the car while he stayed behind, closing windows and locking up. Then he drove us to the nearest pub.

The Ploughman was an old, wood-beamed country pub that looked like the kind you used to see in *National Geographic*. It was packed with farmers' wives who'd had their hair done for the occasion and hoped you'd notice. Entertainment was limited to a dartboard on the back wall and an ancient little man at an upright organ who launched into "Anchors Aweigh" as soon as he heard there were Americans in the house. Outside, dreary rain splattered against the windows; but within we ate baskets of shrimp and chips before a huge, smoldering fireplace, drank the local ale and hummed along with "I'll Be Seeing You" and "The White Cliffs of Dover".

Susan began to fade fast after we ate, so we headed home early. Despite the rain, it was still light out when we dashed through the puddles to the farmhouse. That's why it was so easy to see the computerized pad wired neatly to Edward's back door.

There was a long, hushed moment when nobody spoke or breathed, and then Edward started bellowing, "Get away from the door! Get in my car! Both of you in my car! Keegan, you'll have to drive!"

I heard him, but I was mesmerized by the flashing red and white lights and the wires attached to the door jamb. When he shook my arm and yelled louder, I moved, scrambling into the front seat of the Volvo beside Susan. Then I looked at the right hand steering wheel and slid back out. There was no way I was driving in England; I knew better.

First corner or cross street, and I'd be right back on the U.S. side of the road.

"We all have to go," Susan was insisting. "It's not safe. You can't stay here."

"Get in the car . . . Go!" Edward out-shouted her, his words fragmenting in the wind. "Back to town . . . my mobile phone . . . call the police . . . I want you away . . ."

"Listen." I was pretty much OD-ing on drama. "I can't drive all the way to London on the left hand side of the road. Or in London or in any other English town for that matter. Not unless you want messed up traffic and wrecks galore."

"Of course, you can drive!" Edward was still projecting several hundred decibels above the norm.

I shook my head emphatically, but he didn't notice.

"There's nothing direct to London, you'll have to change in Sheffield. Matlock's only a few miles away and the train station's right in the middle of town. Leave the car in the lot. I'll collect it later and meet you as soon as I've taken care of — this. Don't, under any circumstances, go back to the Abbott or to Keegan's hotel! Go somewhere else, anywhere else and check into the same room together. Don't answer the door! Don't leave the building! Call me when you get there. And get going!"

Edward, roused, was nothing like the laid back photographer I'd interviewed days earlier. He leaned across me, started the engine, and shooed us out of the driveway like wayward chickens, walking straight at the car until I reversed into the lane.

Backing's no problem in England, anybody can do it. I shifted into drive, moved two feet forward and rolled down the window.

"How do we get to Matlock?"

"Oh, God, I forgot. Straight ahead, left at your first opportunity, pass the pub, third right and straight ahead until you see the posting signs. Eight miles. Watch for the turn."

"Okay." I hit the accelerator and we went.

Driving up a narrow lane lined with hedgerows was easy enough; turning left onto the main road was a nightmare. It had grown steadily darker, and rain was slithering down the windshield. I couldn't find the switch for the wipers and head-lights kept flashing up, blurring straight at us out of nowhere at about ninety miles an hour. And that was before we came to the roundabouts.

After driving the wrong way around two of them Abby, I mean, Susan, began shouting more or less nonstop and throw-ing in an occasional shriek for variety. "Left lane! *Left* lane! Keegan! Watch out for that van! Stay left, no, *left*!" There were a lot more instructions, but I was so traumatized I only heard the ear-splitting ones.

When I went roaring through an intersection — on the proper side of the road, I might add — she confused me com-pletely by breaking into sobs. "We missed it. We missed it. The sign said the center of town was right. Oh, God, we missed it!"

"Listen, do you want to drive?" I did a U-turn in the middle of the road that nearly got us broadsided by a car towing a caravan, shot back in the direction we'd come and hung a huge left, throwing Susan over against the passenger door where she landed on her bad arm. That ended the screaming. A few minutes later, she remarked in a subdued voice, "Train station, straight ahead."

We left Edward's Volvo in the car park after feeding enough fifty pee pieces in the slot to keep it in perpetuity and hustled as fast as Susan could move to the ticket booth.

The first part of our headlong flight from reality had been nightmarish; the rest was merely maddening. Matlock to Sheffield to London took three and one-half hours. We were al-ready too late to make that connection. The only other possibility was taking a train to Manchester and changing again in Birmingham, but the Manchester train was leaving in six minutes. We split up, Susan to get tickets, me to get coffees at the station café, and made it to our first class seats with a minute to spare. That was as good as it ever got.

At Manchester we had nine minutes to make our connection but got on the wrong platform by mistake. Frantically we searched for the right one and boarded just seconds before the train pulled out. In Birmingham we threw ourselves on a train that was actually moving out of the station at the time amidst shouting and extremely personal remarks from railroad personnel. If we'd had any luggage at all, we'd still be there, sprawled across the tracks.

Our new train had very comfortable, upholstered seats, but by the time we were London bound, Susan was seriously in pain. She looked like she might throw up. I made a run to the buffet car and returned with lukewarm tea in Styrofoam cups and a pile of paper towels. Susan choked down more pain pills and managed a weak smile. "Lucky I carry a purse everywhere, huh? Even luckier the pills were in it."

I agreed. My purse, passport and clean underwear were all back at the farm. The 10 pounds I'd stuffed in my pocket for the pub, now reduced to six, was my only viable asset.

She must have read my mind. "Edward will bring everything when he comes." She closed her eyes and rested her head against the seat. "I'm sorry about all the yelling. About your driving, I mean. I'm not usually . . ."

"No problem, I was terrified myself. All I could think was I didn't want to die on a road in Derbyshire. The good news is we made it, and I'm sure nobody followed us."

Her eyes popped wider immediately. "I never thought of someone following. I suppose they all know about Edward's place in the country — Nigel, Liz, Josef — even the people at the gallery."

"Probably."

"So, it could be anybody, couldn't it? Even that girlfriend of Josef's or . . a relative who has an interest."

I could see where she was headed, and I didn't like it, but my own thoughts were no better:

Yesterday I'd called Reid, asked for Edward's number and disappeared, leaving a message that I'd be out of town with Mrs. Russell. Edward had dropped out of sight the same day. Not a monumental leap to decide the three of us were somewhere together, and Edward's farm in Derbyshire would be a dandy place to start looking. Still, attaching a bomb to somebody's door was idiotic as well as completely unbelievable. Much better to burn the place down when we were asleep. But who? And why?

How much of the gallery do you actually own?" I said suddenly. "I mean, how much do you think Abby owned?"

"She told me once she put eight thousand in it — pounds. The pound was worth about two eighty U. S. back then, so twenty-two thousand dollars or so. If they got rid of me . . . except they don't know I'm not me — well, not all of them know — it wouldn't mean much financially . . ." Her voice had begun to slur a little, either from the medication or exhaustion.

I wondered what $22,000 in 1966 was equivalent to today. Surely Reid, with his business background, was beyond involvement in anything that stupid, but my past was littered with surely nots. I shifted my thoughts to someone who might be stupid or spiteful enough — Beijing. There was a connection with her and the gallery, some idea that had slipped through my head, something I couldn't retrieve.

"Might even be two of them," Susan was mumbling,

"working together. If they thought . . ." she groaned as she shifted position, "but the . . . bomb . . . that's all right now, isn't it? Edward's out of it. He was with us."

She looked so pathetic, I let it ride, but she was forgetting one small fact: When we left for the pub, Edward's car had been parked out front, and he was the last one out of the farmhouse. If he'd wanted, for whatever insane reason, to stick an exploding device on his own back door, neither of us would have seen him do it.

I decided being cold, damp, bedraggled and possibly suffering from post-bomb, post-driving shock had addled my brain. Maybe they all were guilty, maybe even Susan. I looked across at her. Her head lolled against the headrest, and her eyes were closed. She looked like a bruised child who'd cried herself to sleep. When I folded some of the paper towels into a thick pad and blotted her damp hair and face, she didn't move. I used some paper towels on my own hair, resisted the temptation to stuff a bunch of dry ones under my armpits, drank the rest of the cold tea and tried, unsuccessfully, to get some sleep.

Chapter 20

W e arrived at Euston Station at 1:21 a.m., exactly five hours and nineteen minutes after fleeing Derbyshire. It was raining in London too, cold rain for June, and a miserable night to be looking for a hotel room, particularly when we had no luggage and one of us was discolored, battered and wearing a sling.

The cab driver we picked up at the station was the lucky draw of the night. He was Irish, at least sixty, and looked a little battered himself. He presumed we were fleeing abusive husbands, found an all night pharmacy and waited patiently while I bought toothbrushes, shampoo, deodorant, extra large T-shirts and some really good chocolate. After that, he wasn't so patient. And the problem was me.

My brain was too frazzled to remember any of the places

I'd stayed during the Nineties. The harder I tried, the more the names eluded me.

The cab driver was getting seriously antsy when Susan stirred on the seat beside me, opened her eyes and said clearly, "Helen Graham House, the old YWCA. I went there the day Abby died," she explained, "and it's very safe. Nobody gets past the front desk."

Since she was paying, and I couldn't think of anything better, I said okay, shrugging away the fact that the old Y just happened to be located on the same street as our hotels.

As it happened, Helen Graham House was blocks from where we were staying, but it was a total bust. Not only was it fully booked, it allowed women only 18–30 years old.

Fully booked was a fact of life, but Susan couldn't get past the age thing. The fact that her old refuge was out of reach sent her into a semi-coherent monologue on how much better the old London had been in every decade before the current one. That segued into a longer story about the Forties, her mother and World War II.

"She lived on a little street off Aldersgate. She hid under the porch when the bombing started and the doodlebugs came. She was too claustrophobic to go down the Underground so she slept with a gun . . . with two bullets . . . one for her and one for her sister should the Germans come. And," she turned to look at me, her voice suddenly outraged, "do you know what they did to it?"

I shook my head. "The Germans?"

"No, the English. Built the Barbican over it. The freaking Barbican Performing Arts Center, right over my mother's house. Like it never existed. How could they do that?"

I studied her for a moment in the darkness. "Did you take some more pain pills?"

"A few." Her eyes were slightly glazed. "But I'm all right." She drew in an impatient breath. "It's just that I need this to be over. I don't think I'll ever sleep again unless I get some closure."

"Closure?" I glanced at the cab driver whose shoulders were hunched in an ominous manner. I didn't blame him; I hate the word too. Besides, we'd been parked illegally in front of Helen Graham House for nearly ten minutes.

"Okay, I remember a hotel," I told the cab driver. "Just a few blocks from Victoria Station. Wilford Place."

If it hadn't been for the 40 pounds Susan had already given him, he'd probably have put us out on the street. Instead he pulled away from the curb and roared off to what might be a place he could dump us.

We'd only covered a few blocks when Susan leaned forward and spoke to him. "Please, can you take us past 146 Finborough Road on the way? It's important."

He looked up and caught my eye in the rear-view mirror.

I shrugged and nodded. "Yes, please, we'll make it worth your while."

Fifteen minutes later we pulled up in front of Susan's former flat.

"I'm not getting out," she announced to the driver. "I just wanted to look at it. I used to live here, you see."

I leaned across the seat to peer at the three story brick house. It looked as shabby in the dark as it did in daytime, even through rain-slicked windows, and no lights showed on any of the floors.

"We lived in the basement," Susan's voice was hoarse and a little squeaky, "but Edward's flat was much better. Miles warmer than ours. He had a bar heater that worked and a heated towel rack in the bathroom; sometimes I took baths there. He'd give me a glass of wine and light the fireplace and read bits of his novel out loud. He did all the different voices, even the women." She let out a long, tired breath.

"I used to go up there when the fighting got bad. Nigel and Abby . . . They seemed to hate each other more every day. Edward was a lot more fun, but he was bitter about Abby, too. Said she screwed up people's lives for the fun of it, and somebody should put a stop to her nonsense. He said he'd do it himself and it would be a public service. That was the first thing I thought of when I saw her sprawled on the lounge floor that day."

She took a hard look at the entrance to the basement flat, sighed and slumped back in her seat, "I used to think it was the longest walk from 146 to the tube station, but it's only really about half a block. If I remembered that wrong, maybe I got the rest wrong too." She turned her head in my direction, but her eyes were closed. "If they build a Barbican over the top of 146, would that time — our time — just not exist? Would Abby not be dead anymore?"

"We're finished here," I said to the driver and repeated the address I'd given him earlier.

The residential hotel I'd remembered was no longer a hotel, more like a down at the heels B&B. It looked a lot like 146 Finborough Road.

We dragged ourselves out of the cab, Susan thrust several folded notes through the driver's open window and waved goodbye. The cab, however, didn't move. After a second, our Irish friend leaned out and handed the money back. I could tell he was having an internal struggle.

"I can't take this, ma'am. It's too much."

"Not at all." Susan drew herself up, her voice formal, if slightly slurred. "It's the price of closure. Thank you so much."

He rubbed his nose with the back of his thumb for a few

seconds, muttered, "Ta," and rolled away from the curb.

The man who answered the door at the B&B was a different specimen entirely. He didn't care for Susan's sling, our lack of luggage or our drugstore bags, but after a judicious distribution of more twenty pound notes, he assigned us a room with two beds and its own bath and shushed us all the way up the stairs.

I didn't like the look of him, either. "Better double-lock the door," I said, but Susan had collapsed on one of the beds and wasn't moving.

I checked to make sure she was breathing, locked the door and propped a chair under the knob, even though all the safety experts say that doesn't really work. Then I crawled under the faded duvet to warm up. The room was cold and stuffy at the same time, but I was too tired to get up and open a window.

"Are you still awake?" I said to Mrs. Russell.

"No." Her voice was faint and groggy. "Wha's matter?"

"Nothing. I just wondered how much you gave the cab driver."

"Oh. Two hundred pounds."

"What?" My yawn turned to a gasp, and I sat straight up in bed. "You're out of your mind. Was a quick trip down memory lane worth all that?"

Mrs. Russell, who was old enough to be my mother and a lady in ways I'd never achieve or even consider, chuckled and said clearly, "Fucking A."

Susan Russell and I were back on the train, racing through the cars, screaming for it to stop. But the engine roared through Kings Cross Station without slowing down. Icy rain and gusts of wind blew down the carriages, knocking us off our feet. I grabbed the back of a seat and held on to Mrs. Russell. But she was being slowly sucked out one of the windows. No, wait, it wasn't Mrs. Russell, it was Beijing wearing Mrs. Russell's Chanel boots. Reid appeared suddenly, grabbed Beijing's leg, and pulled her back into the carriage.

"Let her go, you don't even like her!" I screamed.

He didn't answer.

And then she was slipping away, dragging Reid with her, and there was nothing I could do. A tremendous crash of thunder rocked the train, and it rolled, slow-motion, off the tracks, down the embankment and onto its side.

I sat up in bed, heart racing. The table lamp was still on and my watch said I'd only been asleep a couple of hours. Susan Russell wasn't in the other bed, but before I had time to worry about her, she opened the bathroom door and peeked out, cell phone in hand.

Her hair was damp from the shower, and she was wearing one of the drug store T-shirts. "Sorry about the noise; I knocked something off the sink. I was calling Edward but it went to his voice mail." Pause. "So, then I called Steven."

I wondered what scintillating advice Steven had imparted, but I didn't care enough to ask. I was still trying to shake off the dream, still damp and crumpled and something — most likely me — smelled bad. All I wanted was a lot of very hot water and clean clothes.

The B&B's warm water supply held through my shower, after which I donned my own T-shirt, a fetching number with a British flag and the words:

England expects every woman to do her duty.

I did my duty and crawled back in bed. Unfortunately, I was no longer sleepy.

Susan was also wide awake, and for the next hour we sat up talking, swathed in blankets and eating chocolate. It reminded me of our flight to London except we were both cold stone sober, and this time Abby/Susan was telling the truth. She was still a mass of colorful bruises, but her manner was relaxed, almost verging on frivolous. Whatever Steven's advice had been, she was re-living her Sixties memories as if she'd been dying to do it her whole life.

"Josef was great in those days," she insisted. "Helped me sell a few things, gave me advice about painting —"

"At one time I was pretty sure he was Sunni's father," I said. "That was wrong, huh?"

She shifted her arm back in its sling to a more comfortable position. "He was nice to me, that was all."

"Then why did you crumple in a heap when you saw him at the gallery?"

"It wasn't *him*, it was the girl, Beijing," she said firmly. "All I saw was a swath of dark green and red hair and that curlicue necklace. It was a B, of course, but I saw a white D on a green Dartmouth sweatshirt. For a second my brain split into two parts. One part absolutely understood that Abby was dead; the other saw her standing in front of me. Only it was me, too, in a weird way. That sweatshirt was from an old boyfriend of mine, the only thing I ever successfully hid from Tony. I took it with me when I ran away."

"And the headless paintings?"

She made a face. "I experimented with those years ago. Josef didn't approve, thought they showed lack of talent, but I had a thing about it. I can't imagine what prompted him to reproduce my art work — or dress Beijing that way."

"He probably doesn't know, either. What about Edward? Were you crazy about him back then?"

"No. Oh, I don't know. I wasn't in any position . . . it was difficult. Nigel was easier, one of the best friends I ever had. Whatever you did was fine with him. Edward was more intense. He was always clear about what he wanted."

"Edward's a pretty nice guy. What made you marry somebody like Tony?"

She sighed and pulled the blanket up around her ears "My mom was a war bride, and after dad died she stayed in Rhode Island and raised me with no help from anybody. She was wonderful, but there was never enough of anything. The summer I graduated from high school, I started going out to clubs with my friends. That's where I met Anthony Miachi." The green eyes sparkled for a second.

"He was a hot number, fifteen years older than me, a lifetime older when it came to sophistication. He was also connected. Mom never liked him. She got really sick, and when she was gone there was Tony, wanting to take care of me. For almost a year, he did. We went to Italy on our honeymoon, he bought me a fancy car, I had anything I wanted. Still, he liked control.

"I picked up a job in an art store, but he made me quit. He hated it when I painted because I'd get lost in it, hours at a time. The only place he'd let me go was shopping and only in the daytime. I wanted kids. He didn't, and he got a vasectomy. Didn't tell me, but I found out. We started fighting; he started not coming home nights." She let out a long, voiced breath and turned to look at me.

"Can you imagine? There I was, barely twenty, married to a criminal whose best friend was a hit man named Earl. And Earl kept track of me for my husband. I had no family. The only friend Tony let me spend any time with was a cousin of his. She was Italian too, but she liked me and thought he treated me like dirt — and said so.

"Things went from really bad to a whole lot worse. Worse than you could imagine. And then there was this huge crackdown on crime. Tony was arrested on charges of arson. The second I heard I went upstairs, packed a bag, and grabbed that honeymoon passport. I also helped myself to fifteen hundred dollars."

"You mean you had access to a passport and cash all the time?"

"Not exactly, Tony kept what he called 'emergency items' in a locked drawer of his desk."

"Which you broke into?"

She shrugged. "I left him my wedding rings. They were expensive. I figured that was a fair trade. And then, just as I was starting out the front door, Tony's mother called. She said Earl had been arrested too and she was coming to stay with me until Anthony was released. In other words, she was going to watch me until he got out."

"What did you do?"

"After I panicked and threw up for twenty minutes?" A smile lit her bruised face. "I called my friend — the Italian girl — and asked her to meet me at a department store downtown. She didn't even try to talk me out of the crazy plan I had in mind."

"And?"

"I left my car in the department store lot, hid in the store's dressing room until she arrived, and we traded clothes. She took my expensive suede coat and I got her lined raincoat and a floppy hat that shaded my face. One of her friends was waiting near the side door and drove me to Green Airport. I got on the first plane to New York I could find."

"And then to London?"

"No." She shook her head. "A young couple I sat next to on the plane from Providence were going to Luxembourg on

Icelandic Airways. They said it was cheap. I didn't know how long my money was going to last, so I tagged along. Besides, I didn't want to leave a trail straight to London.

"We had engine trouble all the way. Landed in Halifax for repairs and Reykjavik and Glasgow, and I knew God was punishing me for stealing from Tony and being the worst kind of wife. And then somewhere between Glasgow and Luxembourg, I stopped caring. If the plane went down, it went down and all my problems with it. Of course, we landed safely about two in the afternoon. I got a taxi to the train station and said, "London," at every kiosk until somebody gave me a ticket to Oostende. Then I caught the boat train along with a bunch of English Boy Scouts. I was horribly seasick all the way across and the Scout leader felt sorry for me and got me a room at the YWCA because the hotels were all full. That was Helen Graham House, where," her mouth curved into a smile, "you and I are both too old now to flee.

"I thought I was so smart — landing in the middle of Europe where I could disappear in any direction. I forgot England was the first place Tony would look when he got out of jail because of my mother." She leaned back against her pillow. "Anyway, I saw an ad in the classifieds and moved in with Abby and Nigel and met Edward and Josef and Liz. Those were good days mostly, great days, really."

"Until Abby died."

She nodded. "I was sure Tony or Earl had found me, so, I took off again. But I'm not running anymore. I talked it over with Steven, and I'm staying right here until . . ."

"Yeah?"

"Until it's finished. I don't care if anybody gets punished for Abby, I just want to know who it was. There must be old records around, and England has detectives. Will you stay a little longer and help me? Steven says you're my key person, and it won't be long now." She gave me a sideways look. "I think he's right. You certainly saw right through me. What about the rest of them? Any idea at all who it might be?"

"Well, I have a thought," I hedged, "but it's kind of iffy."

Susan's cell rang. She snatched it off the bedside table, listened for a few minutes, then turned to me. "It's Edward. He's finally finished with the police. The bomb wasn't real, just wires and Play Doh in a foil covered shoebox, but it took them hours to find out. They had to bring in experts to take it apart."

I sat up straighter in bed. "That's the stupidest thing I ever heard. Putting a bomb on somebody's door is crazy enough — but a fake one? What for?"

"The neighbors reported a rental car with London plates going down Edward's lane: a man driving, a woman passenger. The police think it was kids, maybe a practical joke. They said it was a very authentic looking fake."

Susan turned back to Edward, repeated our address and made him promise to get some sleep before driving down to London. There was more conversation, mostly cooing and murmuring, but I tuned out because my brain had started working again.

I didn't know who had killed Abby Pell, but I was pretty sure who hadn't. I also thought that Susan's old friends, with the possible exception of Edward, did know. Maybe with the right incentive, one of them could be persuaded to tell the truth. What we needed was a lie detector. My thoughts shifted to the farmhouse, and I interrupted Susan, saying, "Ask him if he'd mind bringing a bottle of Napoleon brandy when he comes."

She looked surprised but relayed the request. When she terminated the call she turned to me. "You're adding brandy to your one iffy thought, right? You think it's Liz, don't you?

Because of the scrapbook."

"Not necessarily, but I think we should talk to her again before we get into detectives. And she might as well have the incentive of her choice, unless you object to the method."

Her head was already moving back and forth. "Not if she knows and never told — poor Liz."

"Poor Liz?"

"You should have seen her back then. You'd never believe she could look like she does now. And they were a spectacular couple. Josef had thick black hair and this dark, handsome face, and enough energy to light up every room he entered. And Liz was ten years younger with natural silver-blonde hair, cut like Twiggy. She wore all the stuff that went with the Sixties face: black eyeliner, heavy mascara, eye shadow, white powder, white lipstick. Her clothes were the latest thing — miniskirts and colored tights and go-go boots and the new wool trouser suits that came out that year.

"But there was always something a little off about their relationship. It was like he was the one man left in the world, and she was a clinger. He didn't like being suffocated, and, of course, Abby was always in there pitching. Josef never really had a chance, to tell the truth. He didn't know it, but his fastest move was too slow for Abby." She sighed and shook her head. "I'm sorry for Liz, always was, but I want this garbage to stop. I want to walk down the street without looking over my shoulder. And get a night's sleep that isn't mostly nightmares."

"Okay." I yawned, snapped off the lamp and burrowed under my duvet.

"And I turned off my phone so nobody can wake us up," Susan added in the darkness.

"Good idea. Mine's still at the farm, which is also good. I

don't want to report to Sunni that her mother and I are on the lam. Ten to one she's been calling every five minutes to see if I've sold her and her unknown father down the river."

No response to that. Either she was already asleep, which was fast work, or she had no comment. I adjusted my pillow and reserved judgment. Susan Russell might be opening the bag on her past, but she hadn't once mentioned the identity of Sunni's real father. Still, I yawned again, the odds were much better now for identifying both him and Abby Pell's murderer. In each case, in my own mind, I had narrowed the field to two.

Chapter 21

Edward arrived around noon, checked in one floor up, and delivered our suitcases and the brandy. We traded our T-shirts for real clothes and patched ourselves together with the help of curling irons, hair spray and make-up.

Susan was still moving as if every bruise had stiffened; just blow-drying her hair had exhausted her. Obviously, the last thing she needed was a train trip to the south of England. I told her to stay put and I'd see Liz on my own.

"I don't like to wimp out again," she protested, but the protest was weak. "At least take Edward; you shouldn't go by yourself."

"Liz isn't dangerous," I argued, "not at her age and weight. And I'll keep in touch." I took my cell phone from the suitcase and stuck it in my pocket. "I've got this."

In the end I dumped stuff out of the canvas carryall I sometimes used as a purse, squeezed the brandy in and went to Victoria Station alone. I left Susan resting atop her duvet with Edward sitting beside her. They returned my good-byes without looking up, and I smiled as I went downstairs. I had a plan that involved more than wallowing in bed all afternoon and looking sappy.

I was waiting in line for a return ticket to Lewes when I realized my mistake. Vintage brandy might be a powerful incentive, but there was another, better one close at hand: Josef's paranoia about the gallery. I phoned Susan, told her my new idea and got her permission to lie like a rug. Then I put Liz on hold and caught a cab for Chelsea.

After all the previous difficulty in corralling Reid's father, I almost laughed when I entered the Jubilee Walk Gallery. Josef was standing big as life at the front desk, fraternizing with the help, accessible as hell.

"I was hoping to catch you." I moved quickly before he did a disappearing act. "I have a message from Abby Russell, a financial message."

The gallerista manning the phones — yet another redhead, — looked more disapproving than the situation required, but Josef told her to carry on and motioned me down the hall to his office. His personal work space was elegant: three walls painted a warm, dark rust, the fourth an enormous jigsaw puzzle of brushed versus shiny copper. He held a black leather chair for me then moved behind his desk to another, slightly larger one.

"Sorry to drop in without calling," I said as he was sitting down, "but I won't take much of your time. Mrs. Russell would like some," I sucked it up and spoke the word for what I hoped was the last time, "closure. Abby isn't Abby, she's really Susan

Miachi, but you know that because you found Abby dead in Nigel's flat. You dress your friend Beijing just like Abby looked that day: long red hair, dark green sleeves, no underwear and an ornate white letter."

Josef had stopped moving ten inches from the chair's seat. By the time he sat completely down, he looked a hundred years old. I went on talking to his closed, gray face. "I couldn't understand why you were worried about the gallery. Susan had no claim on anything and neither did Abby, unless you'd given her something in writing. Like maybe an I.O.U. for eight thousand pounds? Did you search the flat looking for it? Or start a fire to destroy what you couldn't find? Susan carried Abby's backpack away by mistake that day. Did you know that? Passport, clothes, papers, everything."

I waited in case he wanted to say anything, but he didn't seem to be breathing, let alone talking.

"Fortunately for you," I went on, "Susan is more interested in what happened that day than she is in a chunk of the gallery. Was Abby already dead when you got to the flat? Did the two of you have an argument? We know you called the police from the tube station."

I leaned forward in my chair and waited, for anger, resentment, denial, whatever, but Reid's father was so silent he looked catatonic. If he was having a fit, my next stop would definitely be Lewes. Liz and her inventory of ancient grievances might be our only hope.

When Josef straightened suddenly and pulled in a sharp, noisy breath, I almost jumped out of my chair. He leaned across the desk, dark eyes staring straight into mine. "Do you have the — the paper with you?"

"The I.O.U.?" I kept the triumph of guessing correctly off my face. "No, not with me."

He leaned back and transferred the stare to his desk. Two more long minutes went by, and I thought he was refusing the bait. Wrong again. Apparently he was just deciding how to minimize his losses. The gallery, it appeared, won every time.

"I found her on the floor of the lounge." The words were soft, almost a whisper.

I suppressed a smile. Crafty old Josef was keeping his voice too low to be picked up by a recorder, and it hadn't even crossed my mind to tape him.

"Was anybody else in the flat?" I said in normal tone of voice, ignoring his muffled responses.

He shook his head.

"But the living area, the lounge, was torn apart?"

"Yes."

"And her face was battered in? The body burned?"

He shuddered and shifted in his chair. "What did Susan say about that?"

For a second he lost me. Then I said, "You saw Susan on the way to the flat that day?"

"She was in the tube station. Running down the stairs. I didn't realize she saw me as well."

I didn't tell him she hadn't seen him. "Nobody else around? Nobody you recognized?"

"No, not at all. What will Susan — do — with this information?"

"I think it depends on whether somebody tries to kill her again."

"Kill her?" He drew himself up with a look of distaste. "Reid said she had an accident the night of the opening. But surely —"

"More than an accident, and two days ago somebody pushed her out in traffic again. Whoever it is has a very limited repertoire." I leaned forward. "Mrs. Russell wants to know everything that happened that day."

"If I share that information, she won't, er, cause a problem?"

"Not if it's the truth."

Several more seconds drifted by. Finally he spoke, still in that hushed voice that made him sound like he was eating the words. "Liz and I had an argument that morning. She threatened to kill Abby and me, if I left her. She didn't mean it, of course. I said she was imagining things, that I had to go to the continent for the weekend, and she was interfering with business. I was — harsh. She insisted on accompanying me to Victoria and refused to leave the platform until the train pulled away. That meant I had to ride as far as Wrotham. Once there, I turned around and came back to town, but it was nearly two hours before I got to Earls Court. I've said what I found there." His face looked muddy under the gray-streaked hair. "Liz was right, actually; I would have left her for Abby. In time."

"What did you do when you found her?"

"Got out of that horrid flat." The words came out in his normal voice, which he immediately lowered. "Started to take the tube and changed my mind. Walked most of the way home in the rain. Walked for hours, but I couldn't seem to stop. When I got there, Liz was in bed. She didn't say anything, didn't ask why I wasn't in Brussels. We never really spoke again. In one day everything . . ."

When he didn't go on, I said, "What about Nigel? Was he really in Mallorca when Abby died?"

A flicker of irritation showed in Josef's face. "Of course. As far away as possible after he'd done his worst."

"That being?"

He gave a shrug so elegant it almost wasn't there. "Nigel thought Abby spoiled and underhanded. He wanted her unmasked. I believe that was his term. He was always a bit dramatic, even back then. He saw her as the entire problem."

"What did he do ? What was his worst?"

The look of irritation intensified, then faded. "Nothing very much. Caused a fuss, stirred up bad feelings. That sort of thing."

I settled my bag on my shoulder. There was more, but it would probably be easier to get it from Nigel himself. I stood up and said, "I'll call you after I've spoken to Mrs. Russell."

"And she'll send me the I.O.U.? As promised?" He got slowly to his feet and leaned against his desk, as if for support.

"If the information is correct. Is that all you care about? This gallery?"

His eyes, old and haunted, slid past mine. "It doesn't disappoint."

For a second I was almost sorry for him, but, hey, we're all haunted by something. "Last chance to tell me about Nigel."

He shook his head and continued to shelter behind the desk.

I nodded, turned away, let myself out into the hallway and walked straight into Reid.

My heart tightened, but I didn't speak, not even hello, because I wasn't sure where Reid fit exactly into the scheme of things.

He wasn't looking too sure about me, either, but he didn't share my loss for words. "I called 'round the hotel as agreed, but you'd gone missing. Personally," his voice dropped to a murmur, "I didn't think the sex was all that bad."

I could feel heat creeping up my neck and into my face. "I left a message saying I had to go out of town, that I'd call you later."

"You weren't going out of town the last time I saw you, just to breakfast. What message?"

The thought of our last morning together was warming a lot of other things besides my face. Consequently, I was less articulate than normal; in fact, I stuttered. "Ah, some kind of weird things happened. Somebody pushed Mrs. Russell in front of another taxi, and she had to go to hospital, and then somebody attached . . ."

"Is that why you called me for Edward's number?" he interrupted. "Why didn't you say?"

"I didn't know then. And anyway, you were busy. Moving furniture or something."

"You could have called later, as promised in the message you supposedly left."

I don't like arguing with anybody I've seen naked and would like to see naked again, but it had been a long couple of days and placating arrogant men hadn't made my to-do list for years. "Hey," I said, "Mrs. Russell had a sprained arm and a lot of bruises, and she was scared to death. Getting her out of town seemed like a good idea, although it didn't turn out that way." I stopped, remembering what it was about the gallery that had eluded me. "Where's Beijing's Irish bomb display — the one with the sod and all the wires?"

"I don't know." He looked at me like I'd slipped a cog. "Possibly where it's supposed to be?"

"I don't think so. I think it's up in Derbyshire, attached to Edward's back door."

"What the hell are you talking about?"

"It's funny that all the roads seem to lead to Jubilee Walk, isn't it? From the person who murdered Abby Pell in 1966 to whoever wanted Susan Miachi Russell creamed by a bus this week."

Reid opened his mouth to protest, paused and began decoding my actual words. "What is it you're saying? That Susan didn't . . . that Abby Russell is really Susan Miachi? Abby Pell is the one who died in the Sixties?"

"That's it."

"But I don't believe it. My father . . . somebody would have
. . . but even if . . . none of that has anything to do with us, with
the gallery. Except now —"

I walked away before he finished the thought, took a right
and headed to the room with the real Erin the Free display.

The pieces of sod, now turning yellow-brown, were still there,
but the explosive device that had been attached to them wasn't.

I didn't say anything, and Reid, who had followed me, took
a thoughtful look and merely grunted. Then he followed me to
the reception desk.

Dmitri-the-gofer and the redheaded gallerista were having a
spat. Phrases like stupid cow, blonde American bitch, and total,
total cretin hovered in the air around them, and neither of them
paid us any mind until I was almost in the girl's face.

"I'm Keegan Shaw," I said. "I left a message here a couple
of days ago — around two in the afternoon."

The redhead wrenched her attention from Dmitri and
looked embarrassed and furious all at once. "Sorry, I wasn't
here that day."

"Sure you were." I grinned at her. "I recognize your voice."

"The message was for me, Lorna." Reid spoke from behind
me. "Something about Ms. Shaw going out of town."

"Oh, that. Of course, yes. You were out and I gave it to
Dmitri to deliver. He must have forgotten." She rustled around
under the desk, making patting noises. "Sorry, here it is."

Dmitri's face was so dark I was afraid he'd have a stroke.
His mouth wanted to say, "Liar," but it didn't have the guts.

Reid took the crumpled paper, gave each of them an assessing look and steered me toward the exit.

"Sorry," he said at the front door. "Lorna and Dmitri used to
be an item. He dropped her for some blonde American he met recently. Lorna claims the girl used him and then disappeared, and

he insists Lorna's destroying his messages. They've been at it all morning. Do you have time for a coffee or are you on your way out of town again?"

"I am, actually." I looked at my watch which now showed four o'clock. "Going down to Lewes. But it may have to wait until morning. I want to see Nigel first."

"Nigel?" He hesitated, then took my arm and walked me across the street to a small outdoor café.

When we were seated with a couple of lattes, he picked up the conversation where he'd left it. "Let's see, Nigel — Lewes, which means Liz — and you've just been talking to Josef. You're telling everyone that Abby isn't really Abby, is that it? To see how they react?"

"Something like that."

He eyed me a few moments longer. "And you're sure this is true because she told you so herself? Is that it?"

"Actually I guessed, but she's admitted it. And I have a picture, an old one taken of her in California at the commune." I didn't mention I'd forgotten to show it to anybody.

"All right then." He drew in a breath and let it out. "Now, who would be idiotic enough to fasten the gallery's faux bomb to Edward's farmhouse?"

"I don't know. It happened while we were at the pub. And Beijing's own personal art work is certainly missing."

"Makes no sense at all." He frowned and stirred foam into his coffee.

"I know." I watched him sip the latte and wished we were someplace not so public. You can't lick foam off somebody else's mouth in public. He looked up suddenly and grinned. I got a grip.

"The blonde Dmitri was seeing?" I ventured. "Was she with him at the gallery? The night I met you?"

"Possibly. She's been around for at least a week according

to Lorna. A bit wraith-like apparently, disappearing and reappearing at odd times."

"And when did she stop calling Dmitri?"

He shrugged. "Yesterday, I suppose. He wasn't complaining 'til this morning."

"Did you ever see this blonde and Beijing around at the same time?"

He leaned back in his chair and cocked his head at me. "Now that is a stretch. Anyway, she wouldn't do that."

"Why not? Because she told you so herself?" I eyed him across the table, remembering my weird dream. "Were you and Beijing an item too at one time?"

The corner of his mouth twisted. "Let's just say I knew her first."

"All right then."

"You misunderstand. She wouldn't do it because she's not clever enough to either think of it or pull it off."

"Maybe not, but she obviously knows how to dress up as someone else. A wig makes a huge —" I stopped talking.

Beijing, wearing an armful of copper bracelets and a white shirt open nearly to the waist was coming down the street. She was talking furiously into her cell phone when she passed within inches of our table without noticing we were there. Her mouth was pressed so hard against the phone only three words were intelligible: "Damn you, Dmitri."

Chapter 22

Fifteen minutes later, Reid and I separated. He went back to the gallery, and I went to meet Nigel at a restaurant in the East End. I took a cab to the place, a mom and pop café specializing in pie and mash.

I had phoned Nigel before I left Reid, which was lucky. Otherwise Nigel would probably have refused to see me. First, he was too busy, then he was too tired, and finally he didn't have anything to add to what he'd already told me. Eventually, Reid took the phone out of my hand, spoke for a couple of minutes, and Nigel agreed reluctantly to meet for what he referred to as an early nosh.

He wasn't around when I got there. I sat at a table in the back, ordered a platter of chips from the waitress and pondered the Beijing-Dmitri connection. The girl was undoubtedly a hot number, and Dmitri, like a lot of young guys, probably enjoyed wrestling out of his age and weight class. Had he enjoyed it so much he'd let her talk him into driving a phony bomb to Derbyshire? It was so over-the-top, so easily traced to the gallery, I couldn't imagine what either of them hoped to gain.

My chips, hot, greasy and perfect when salted and soaked in malt vinegar, were gone by the time Nigel arrived. The waitress followed him to my table where he ordered cottage pie and a pot of tea without looking at the menu. I told her I'd have the same; I was still hungry and wasn't sure when my next meal would be.

Nigel slumped in a chair, loosened his purple tie and eyed me without enthusiasm. "I give up, Americano. Why this critical — and inconvenient — meeting?"

"I have a couple of questions. They're important, and this time I need the truth."

"Darling," his eyebrows rose in mock concern, "why so fierce? The truth about what?"

I looked into his eyes and saw only fatigue and resentment. Probably the easy way wasn't going to work. "Tell you what," I offered. "I'll go first. One, I'm not really writing an article about Susan Miachi's death, and two, Susan isn't dead. She's been pretending to be Abby since 1966."

I should have just punched him in the stomach.

His mouth opened, his eyes scrunched up and he stopped breathing as his face flushed crimson. Before I could Heimlich him, he began to choke out words. ". . . should have known . . . did know at some level . . . too nice, *this* Abby, too much like Susan might have been when she grew up . . ."

The waitress, whose sense of timing couldn't have been worse, padded up just then with a teapot, a jug of milk and a crusted sugar bowl. By the time she took her sorry-self away, Nigel was breathing evenly and his color was better.

He poured out two mugs of tea with only a slightly unsteady hand, sugared his heavily and took his time sipping it.

"In a way, it's a great relief," he said finally, in a more controlled voice, "although I suppose one mustn't indulge in unfettered rejoicing. But why trek all the way down here? You could have rung me up."

"True, but there's more." I told him about Susan's second accident, the one in front of the Wolseley, and he seemed genuinely astonished. "Who would do that?" he said, then answered himself, "Nobody!"

"How about somebody who knew Susan returned to the flat early and discovered Abby's body?"

"Susan was there? Good Lord. That's why she's here after all this time."

He poured himself more tea, sipped it, and thought about it for a second. "What does she plan to do?"

"Josef asked me that very thing just this afternoon."

"He's known all along, hasn't he? Knew it wasn't Abby, and he let me get —" Nigel's lips tightened. "What did he tell you?"

"Not much. That he pretended he had a business trip but was really meeting Abby. That Liz insisted on accompanying him to the train and made him late getting to Earls Court. That Abby was dead when he finally got to 146. He also mentioned how angry you were about him and Abby, and how you —"

"How I what?" he snapped, leaning back, arms folded across his chest.

I shook my head. "It's too late to go on pretending. I don't want Susan Miachi to die this time, either, especially not because of a forty-year-old mistake. Do you?"

He didn't answer.

"Actually you don't have to tell me. It isn't that hard to figure out. Abby plans a weekend with Josef. She gets rid of Susan by sending her to Coventry, and the very same weekend you take off suddenly for Mallorca with friends, leaving her a clear field." I leaned a little forward. "You found out they were meeting at the flat and you told Liz. You set them up and then made sure you were out of town."

The waitress materialized beside our table, removed the lid from the pot, poured a pitcher of hot water slowly into it, replaced the lid, rearranged the milk jug and trundled away.

"You win." I picked up my purse. "I'm out of here. Do you pay that woman to run interference? Is there a buzzer under the table?"

"Wait." He put out a hand, his voice tired and resigned. "It's not what you think. Abby didn't care what happened to anybody as long as she got what she wanted. She was taking drugs, partying all the time, bonking guys in bathrooms or closets or in plain sight at the clubs. Trying to punish Josef for not choosing her faster. For a while she never ate, slept or shut up. She was totally self-absorbed, spiteful, jealous and bloody brilliant at getting you to do what suited her." He sucked in a disgusted breath. "Josef could never see it, and I'd finally had enough. I merely let Liz have my key to the flat and made sure I was far away and surrounded by friends. I admit I hugged myself the entire time, imagining severe beatings and Abby finally getting her comeuppance, the selfish bitch."

"But Liz killed her instead?"

He shook his head. "I don't know that and neither do you. I went to see her when I got back from Spain. She was scratched up, bruised all over. She wouldn't talk; she just lay in bed and stared holes through me. I didn't even ask if she went to the flat, let alone used the key. I went away, down to Cornwall, and when I came back to London, Josef and Liz had split. I haven't seen her since, except that day by accident with Edward." He stared down at the table. "Susan and Abby were so totally different. I wish I could make you understand."

He rubbed his forehead with the back of his hand.

"There was a party in Golders Green, the most poisonous people, entirely over the top. LSD cubes scattered about like bowls of crisps and actual piranhas kept in an aquarium. I got there late, just in time to see them swishing their cat through the aquarium and shouting, 'Kitty want to swim!' The cat already had a stubby, nearly non-existent tail. There was also a baby, a very thick looking baby, sitting in the corner with absolutely no expression, and I was petrified they'd take it for a swim too."

I shuddered, as much at the tone of his voice as at the story.

"The host was albino, white hair and skin like Andy Warhol, only not as handsome, and he took me upstairs. There was Abby, starkers, all catatonic and staring eyes on somebody's unmade bed. She was a disgrace. I got her dressed and into a cab, but she kept trying to jump out or curl into the fetal position. The cabbie nearly threw us out in the rain. When we finally got home, she stood naked in our deadly cold bathroom all night, looking at herself in the mirror and muttering that she could see thousands of Abbys stretching into infinity. I would have let the silly cow freeze, but Susan," his voice cracked suddenly, "put our only bar heater in the bathroom, which meant the bedroom was like ice. And then she crawled in with me, and I warmed up her hands and feet, and held her until she went to sleep."

He looked up and met my eyes at last.

"I couldn't imagine Susan pregnant, but the dead girl was — and Abby was supposed to have had an abortion. If I hadn't told Liz — I shouldn't have told Liz — I loved Susan, I really did."

The waitress re-appeared with steaming plates of cottage pie, one for Nigel, the other for me.

I ate mine.

I was late catching the train to Lewes, and it was nearly dusk before I reached Liz's cottage. That gave me plenty of time to wonder if she was even home and if I should have risked a call ahead.

Her front door was answered by a woman I'd never seen before. She introduced herself as the next door neighbor and led me out to the back garden where Liz sat tucked up in a blanket on a chaise lounge. A mobile phone lay on the table beside an empty glass.

She didn't seem surprised to see me, and I wondered if she'd been fielding calls from Josef or Nigel. The neighbor, whose name was Moira, announced that she was off to make tea and disappeared into Liz's house.

I sat down, uninvited, in a garden chair and put my bulging canvas bag on the ground beside me. Liz wasn't looking good. Without makeup, her skin was pasty with red veins and numerous brown spots. She wore a blonde wig today, a medium length, flippy one that changed shape every time she moved her head.

She frowned at me and my bag. "What do you want now? At this time of evening?"

"Mrs. Russell got the scrapbook you left," I said to her. "To me that meant you were ready to talk about 1966."

Her face went blank for a second, then, "Well, they're all talking now, aren't they? *Their* versions of what we did and the way things were. Even the famously closed-mouthed Josef. How did you manage that?"

"Not easily. He says the two of you argued at the gallery the day Abby was murdered, and that you threatened to kill them both."

She inclined her head and the wig shifted a little. "I over-reacted, I expect. He wanted children, and I couldn't have them.

She could. He kept saying we should try to come to some kind of compromise."

"What sort of compromise?"

"A ménage a whatever, I suppose. He said," her voice became a pompous version of Josef's, "these things were *better arranged* by the French. I told him what I thought of that."

"So you insisted on seeing him off to Brussels?"

"He swore he wasn't meeting her; I wanted to watch him actually get on the train. He did, squirming all the while."

There was the sound of footsteps and the neighbor appeared on the garden path with a tray. She put it down and stood by the table, obvious interest in her eyes.

"Thank you, Moira." Liz sounded less than grateful. "We can manage now."

"I can stay and do the washing up . . ."

"No, you've done quite enough. Thank you."

Moira smiled and backed reluctantly away.

"I've kind of overdosed on tea today," I said, reaching down into my bag and pulling out the bottle of brandy, "Edward sent this. He thought you might like it."

"Did he?" Her eyes were as flat as her voice as she registered the lie. Still, she took the bottle, opened it and poured brandy into our cups. She topped hers with tea, drank it down and refilled the cup, this time without tea.

"Funny, isn't it? Edward's always had a way about him. Charming enough to hide the fact that he always got what he wanted; intelligent enough to get away with — well, murder. He hides his temper well, doesn't he?" She paused. "No one would guess now how furious he was when Abby — well, anyway, I hope you and Mrs. Russell are being very careful."

I tried not to visibly react, but I was frozen to my chair. Edward? Edward who was alone with Susan in a place nobody knew about except the three of us? Edward? Her eyes locked into mine over the rim of her cup, enjoying the jolt she'd given me. Her smile got wider.

After a second I smiled back, in spite of the sweat trickling down my back. "Come on, Liz, don't waste my time. We both know it wasn't Edward. Or Josef."

"Or poor pathetic Nigel?" She cocked her head. "You've figured it all out, have you? It's like a dream sometimes, like it never happened. And then I go to sleep, and there she is, rubbing it in my face, standing there in Susan's green shirt with her bare bum hanging out, laughing at me because she's waiting for *my* husband. I was just going to hit her, black her eye for her so she wouldn't look so sexy, when Josef finally turned up, but she didn't care a damn about that, either. She was waving around a handwritten note to prove she had a stake in the gallery and telling me about changes *they* was going to make. She hadn't got the abortion at all and when she told Josef that, she said he'd leave me for her. And I knew he would, though it probably wasn't even his child. I grabbed the easel and hit her until the sneer left her stupid, insolent face."

Liz shifted on the chaise lounge, reached a shaky hand for the cup of brandy and drank.

"When Susan turned up, I'd got a shirt out of the bedroom and somebody's jacket because mine were — all over blood. I was in the bathroom cleaning up when she started fumbling at the front door. I should have killed her too. I could have at that point, but I didn't want to get messed up again."

She laughed, a small soft sound. "It doesn't matter what I say to you, does it? They didn't keep DNA back then, not in 1966, so there's no evidence. Thank God for telly."

She stared into her empty cup. "The truth is, she got what she deserved. I flushed Josef's handwritten I.O.U. down the toilet and put my clothes in a paper bag and got out as fast as I could. Susan wasn't in sight; she must have run all the way to the tube station. Funnily enough, though, I did see Josef. I was going down the escalator to the trains, and he was coming up just opposite. It made me laugh that he was getting soaked to the skin to be with that cow. And I laughed even harder at what he'd find when he got there.

"Afterwards Nigel was so manic when he returned to London, and Josef didn't speak to me at all, and I was taking pills to sleep and pills to wake up. I didn't understand when the papers said there was a fire. There was no fire; I'd have remembered. I saved all the articles and read and reread them, and I began to think I'd got it wrong. Maybe it really was Susan. Maybe she was hiding in the flat and came out when Abby and I started to argue. Maybe I'd blacked out somehow and struck Susan, and Abby ran away and never came back. But last week, when she came down here and sat in my garden, I knew it was Susan. So Abby was well and truly gone — and I didn't need clippings anymore. Edward had told me where she was staying. I went straight along."

"But why give them to Susan?"

She shrugged and hitched the blanket closer around her knees. "Why not? She was poking her nose in after all this time. And it was her story, too. I was giving her a chance at it."

"And part of you wanted her to know the truth?" When she didn't answer, I said, "Then why push her in front of a cab the next morning? And how did you even know she was in town that first night at the gallery?"

She raised her chin and stared at me. "You're much stupider than I expected. I dropped the clippings at her hotel and went straight to the train station. I've been here ever since."

She swept the blanket aside and displayed a leg set solidly in a plaster cast. "I fell on my front doorstep that very night and broke my ankle. I'm not supposed to put any weight on it for another week. And for your information," she gave me a smug smile, "I've been waiting nearly fifty years to say those things out loud to somebody who didn't matter. The brandy was unnecessary, though I appreciate the thought and effort you put into it."

"My pleasure." I kept my voice calm even as I stood up and collected my bag. "And for your information, Josef set the fire at the flat. He might have been finished with you at that point, but he did try to destroy the evidence. He did try to protect you, even after what you did."

"Not me," her smile stayed in place, but her wig twitched back and forth, "the bloody gallery."

I left the cottage and crossed the street to the neighbor, who must have been glued to her front window. The door opened the second I rang, and Moira was there. "Does Liz need me again? Is she ready to get into bed?" she asked.

"I expect so. How long has she been injured?"

"Oh, since late Tuesday night. Dreadful thing, she fell as she got out of the taxi. They wanted her to stay in hospital, but she wouldn't. The district nurse comes in to help with baths, but I make her tea and fetch anything she needs. Not much of a neighbor if you can't help a neighbor."

I skipped a taxi and walked the mile to the station because I wanted to think. Liz might have beaten Abby Pell to death in 1966, but she obviously hadn't been in London throwing Mrs. Russell under a cab two days ago.

Chapter 23

The London train was nearly empty. I turned on my phone, called Reid to say where I was, and turned it back off. I didn't feel like talking to anybody else. I didn't feel anything, which made no sense at all. I now knew the outcome, knew who had killed Abby Russell. Where was the sense of elation? The rush of guessing right?

Well, nearly right. In my mind I had narrowed Abby's killer to Liz or Nigel, simply because they hated her the most. Bashing in somebody's face requires the hate factor. But I was also sure that Susan Russell's problems would be over once we knew the truth, and that wasn't the case.

I slid off my shoes and propped my feet in the empty seat across from me. If not Liz, then who? Who still wanted to hurt Susan Russell? And what kind of mind was willing to wait this long for the opportunity?

I stared at my reflection in the dark windows as the miles flew by, thinking back to my first conversation with Mrs. Russell. Then I visualized each of the people involved and replayed those conversations in my head, word for word. Then I went back and did it again.

And after another forty-five minutes and two stops, I saw what we'd missed and felt even worse than before. Nobody wants to know an answer if that answer can destroy you all by itself. Especially not Mrs. Russell. And I didn't want to be the one who had to tell her.

It was after midnight when I reached the B&B. Susan and Edward were still up. Susan was now bundled under her duvet with a box of tissues and what appeared to be the onset of a killer cold.

Edward was sitting beside her in the room's only chair, and he rose as I entered. I waved him back and perched on the edge of her bed and reported my conversations with Josef and Nigel fully, but when I got to Liz, I snapped on the tiny recorder and let them hear for themselves. I might have forgotten to tape Josef, but I hadn't forgotten Liz.

Edward was upset about my use of his name and his brandy — right up until he heard Liz suggest he'd gotten away with murder. When he heard her admit to killing Abby, he was stunned, though he must have seen it coming. Susan seemed more resigned, but she was coughing and blowing her nose every few seconds and obviously running a fever.

I had to explain the timing on Liz's broken leg twice so they'd realize she hadn't pushed Susan in front of a cab (at least not the second time) or planted the fake bomb on the farmhouse.

"I don't understand how somebody got it out of the gallery unnoticed," Edward protested. "And to what purpose?"

I shrugged. "No clue as to purpose, but I expect Dmitri removed it. He was in and out all the time carrying plastic wrapped pieces of art, and Erin The Free was in that small, separate room. I don't think bomb art draws much of a crowd."

"Still . . . " Edward got up and began pacing the room, hands stuffed in the back pockets of his jeans, blue eyes worried.

After several minutes of depressed silence, Susan sent him off to his own room, saying she didn't want to give him her cold and she'd call when she felt better. He didn't argue, kiss her good night, or look either of us in the eye. He merely waved a hand from the doorway and wandered away.

Susan blew her nose and said, "You should go too, Keegan, I'll just keep you up all night, and you might catch this flu — cold — whatever it is. Ask the night manager to find you another room."

"Actually, I've made other plans, if you're sure you don't mind being by yourself."

"No." Her voice was so nasal it hurt to hear it. "I'm too miserable to give a damn and nobody knows where I am anyway. I just can't imagine — who the hell's doing this?"

"Well, Liz was right about one thing," I told her, moving to Edward's empty chair. "I have been stupid, not only about the photo of you and Gerry at the commune, but about Dmitri and his girlfriend, Nigel, Josef, everybody. I had a lot of time to think on the way back to town, and I'm pretty sure I understand who and why, but if I'm right, you may want to reconsider your need to know the truth."

Her head moved slowly back on forth on the pillow. "It's too late for that. I want to know."

"You have to be absolutely positive. What's your worst nightmare?"

She started to answer but got derailed by another coughing

fit. When that passed she lay still with her eyes closed for a long time. Then she said in a small voice, "It wouldn't . . . it couldn't be."

"I think it could. I think it's the answer."

Her lips pressed together, deepening the creases around her mouth. "Not possible."

"If it were, would you rather face it now or just hope it didn't happen again sometime in the future?"

"Oh, God, it can't be." She blinked twice then covered her eyes slowly with both hands. "Love is never what it's supposed to be, is it? Oh, God. I can't do . . . even the mildest confrontations. I always get talked out of it. God, I'm a total wuss, still that pathetic girl who runs away when things get tough. No guts."

I reached out and patted her arm. "Come on, Susan. The first time you ran away you were nineteen years old, pregnant and living with a bunch of crooks. Instead of taking an overdose, you left the country in three hours flat and started over with no friends or family in sight. The second time, you were ducking a husband you thought murdered your friend. You had guts all over the place."

Susan Russell goggled at me for several seconds, then laughed, coughed and started crying all at once. After a while she said, "You know what I really hate about getting old? The things you love don't have the same — potency — anymore. Lobster dripping with butter doesn't taste as succulent; sex isn't as orgasmic as you remember; joy isn't a guaranteed high. But the things you fear stay just as strong, just as bitter. And they're always there, aren't they? Waiting in the dark for the second sleepless night or too many scotches."

I handed her another box of tissues from the night stand. "This isn't like before. There's a difference between running away and absenting yourself for a time for self-protection."

"Thank you." She managed a tiny smile.

I got to my feet and stood on the threadbare carpet. "Maybe you should talk to Steven. See what he suggests."

"I already know; he was very clear. I just didn't understand. Now I do. Would you . . ." her voice cracked and she cleared her throat, "could you do one last thing for me? I'm just hanging on here, Keegan, I've got nobody else to ask."

I hesitated, remembering the hard, in-your-face lessons I'd learned about helping versus enabling, but they seemed a little academic now. This woman was too sick, too alone and too banged-up, physically and emotionally, to manage by herself. It wasn't my job, I was clear about that, nevertheless . . .

"I'll do it for Susan Miachi," I said at last. "Tell me what you want done and how."

When I left the room fifteen minutes later, I carried an overnight bag and a page of handwritten notes. Mrs. Russell's instructions were surprisingly coherent, considering the flood of tears that had accompanied each paragraph. I had promised to carry them out.

I also promised to call her daughter Sunni that night before I went to bed.

"I know I said I'd tell her about her father," Susan said, "but I can't right now."

"You sure you don't want me to stay here tonight? It's not a problem."

"No, I need to be by myself and there's nothing to be afraid of any more, is there? I'll bolt the door after you go and, unless I see your number, I'll ignore the phone. I'll be all right."

I wasn't sure of that, but I wasn't sure anything I was doing was right. Something kept prodding me, pushing me forward. Maybe it was Steven, putting a whammy on me from faraway California.

I waited outside in the hall until I heard Susan dead-bolt the door, then trudged downstairs and out to the curb. Reid's shiny black car was waiting there, as agreed. The passenger door swung open and I got in, tossed my bag on the floor and slouched into the seat. Reid gave me a long look before leaning across the console and gathering me up. His arms were warm and tight, and one hand cradled the back of my head. He didn't say stupid things or, in fact, anything at all. After a while I stopped feeling so cold, depressed and alone.

Reid's flat was on the other side of Hyde Park in Bayswater. As we drove there, I recounted my conversation with Nigel, then Liz and finally with Susan Russell and the action she had decided to take. He listened without comment, until he heard my plan for the following day; then he made a suggestion.

"You'd better have me as back up. Going down to Lewes to confront an injured old woman is one thing; this is something else entirely."

"You don't want to be involved," I assured him. "It's nasty and depressing, but nothing will happen to me."

"Just the same." His voice was somber. "I won't interfere, and I'll stay out of sight. Consider it payment in kind for clearing up the mess over the gallery. Maybe now — maybe tomorrow when it's over — Josef can get some peace." He glanced across at me. "I never believed my father was capable of murder, not even in his younger, more volatile days, but I have to admit I'm relieved."

I nodded, searched out my cell phone and punched in a number.

"I promised Mrs. Russell I'd call her daughter, one more thing I'm not looking forward to."

Sunni Russell answered on the first ring. She was livid, furious, irate, pissed off and quite a lot more.

"Where the fuck have you been, Keegan? Your phone's been off for days. Where's my mother? What the fuck's going on?"

I didn't blame her for being angry, but I was too tired and too bummed to offer an explanation. When she finally stopped ranting, I said, "I have the information about your father if you still want it. Are you serious about flying over here?"

A sharp intake of breath echoed all along the line. "Of course I want it." Long pause. "You did it. You actually did it! Sorry. Sorry I lost it. I was just in such a panic, imagining all kinds of horrible things. I'll get on a plane tonight. Miami — that's a better connection than Palm Beach. Tom will drive me down." She seemed to be thinking aloud. "I should be there by early afternoon — before two o'clock, your time. Shall I meet you at the Saxon? Or the Abbott?"

"No, not there, somewhere more . . ." I caught myself up. Her mother was safe enough for the moment; better not alarm Sunni too much. I'd had enough raw emotion for one day. "How about the Oxo Tower? Any cab driver will know where it is, unless you get one who doesn't speak English. In that case, tell him Bankside, south of the Thames. Come up to the bar on the roof. I'll explain why later."

"Sounds pretty cloak and dagger," she laughed uncertainly, "but I'll be there. Will he? My dad, I mean? Is everything okay with him?"

"Well, it's tricky, but I'll explain when I see you. I'm turning off my phone now. I've got to get some sleep."

I ended the call and punched in Susan's number. Nobody answered. After nine rings, I got panicky and redialed. This time she picked up immediately.

"Sorry, Keegan," her voice was so congested it sounded like someone else. "I was in the bathroom."

"Okay. I called Sunni. She says she'll fly out of Miami tonight and be here tomorrow afternoon. I'm meeting her at the Oxo Tower around two, and then I'll tackle the other thing, as we discussed. In the meantime, don't answer your door, not even if someone yells fire, and if you change your mind about . . ."

"No." I waited while she worked through another coughing fit. "I'm not up to any more gut wrenching revelations. About Sunni — just tell her who I really am."

"Her father too? That's really why she's coming."

Silence. Then, "God, I don't know . . . better wait. I'm sorry, Keegan, putting this on you. Am I making another mistake? Handling it like this?"

"I can't think of any other way."

A long sigh. "That's what I thought." She disconnected.

Before I turned off my phone for good, I made one last call. It was late, but I was pretty sure Nigel would still be wide awake. He was, and he listened carefully to the message I gave him.

Reid's flat had leather sofas, a wide screen TV and not a single old master, tottery antique or object d'art in sight. He had promised me a hot bath, a large glass of red wine and a long soothing back rub. I got it all, and a couple of other perks besides. Then I slept like a baby until he woke me around ten the next morning, and we repeated the perks. By one p.m. we were across town finishing up coffee and croissants at a café near St. Paul's Cathedral.

When Sunni phoned to say she was at Heathrow and would

be with me in an hour, max, I was impressed and told her so. An unexpected overnight flight, the inevitable jet lag and here she was, headed straight to our meeting instead of checking into a hotel for a nap or a cleanup. She giggled out loud like a little girl. "I cleaned up on the plane. I want to see my dad."

Reid paid the check, and we crossed the Millennium Bridge to the Tate Modern and walked along the river to the Oxo Tower. I made a quick stop at an ATM for cash, and we arrived just before 2:00 p.m.

Reid camped out at the inside bar while a waiter showed me to one of the small tables on the terrace. I sat in an open weave, yellow plastic chair, felt the sun on my face and watched the police boats glide up and down the Thames. The waiter brought a menu and a glass of white wine, which I was sipping when my phone rang. I expected to hear Sunni say she was running late, but it was Tom Roddler.

"Hey, Keegan." His voice was warm, the voice he used when he wanted you to think he gave a damn. "How've you been? I tried to call a couple of times, but you must have had your cell turned off."

"You could have left a message."

"Not good at messages, better in person. Anyway, it's been a while, and I heard you found somebody you'd rather spend time with than me."

"Really? Where would you hear something like that? Seen Sunni lately?"

"Not for a couple of weeks."

"Not how she tells it," I hadn't meant to say it, but out it came. "Didn't you see her last night?"

"She's not my type, Keegan. I don't need somebody prancing around in a Barbie outfit to get me motivated." He laughed, charm oozing from his end of the connection to mine and forcing a smile in spite of my skepticism. "I'd rather have a real blonde girl who doesn't *yes* me all the time. In fact, one who never *yesses* me."

"Mhhh, right, ... Uh, can I call you back? Something's come up."

Sunni had arrived.

Chapter 24

Sunni Russell was approaching my table with a dark green duffle bag slung over her shoulder. She was dressed in a man's white shirt, lime green clam diggers and matching sandals. Her long red hair had been chopped off and spiked, and she looked like a younger version of her mother.

I put the phone down as she dropped into the chair opposite me. "How was your flight?"

"Not bad." She yawned like she meant it. "Kinda tired. Can't sleep on planes."

"Neither can your mom. I like your hair; it makes you look like her."

She didn't respond to that, just pushed her bag under the table and looked around for a waiter. One appeared, beaming at her, and she ordered a glass of French sauterne. "Want another?" she motioned at my mostly full glass.

"Not yet."

She glanced around at the tables on the rooftop, then through the glass windows dividing us from the rest of the restaurant. She looked older today, in spite of the short hair, and a little jaded. Jet lag will do that.

"Well, is he meeting us here? And where the hell's my dear mother?"

"Wait until your drink comes. You're probably going to need it."

She frowned at me, then shrugged. When the sauterne came, she swallowed a quarter of it and sat back. "Okay, I'm fortified. What's the deal?"

I took in a long breath and took the plunge. "Your mother is really an American named Susan Miachi. The real Abby Russell was murdered here in London in 1966, and your mother took her name and ran away. She ended up at the commune outside San Francisco, married your stepfather and stayed in California for forty-plus years."

Sunni was floored. With these few details the blood in her face went south. "No way," she gasped in a hoarse little voice. Then louder, "No fucking way."

"It's true. "

"Then why isn't she here telling me this? If it's really the truth, where the fuck is she?"

"She asked me to tell you."

Sunni's face twisted into something closer to a sneer than hurt feelings. "And what are you? The daughter she's always wanted?"

"No, she's afraid to talk to you. She's afraid you'll push her off the roof."

The sneer vanished, and she actually looked at the wall

surrounding the patio area before turning back to me with a puzzled look on her face.

"Did you come straight here from the plane?" I asked, holding her gaze. "No stops along the way?"

"No." The puzzled look grew more pronounced. "Why?"

"Let me see your passport."

"My passport! Why?"

"So that I can see you weren't in London last week pushing your mother in front of various taxicabs."

She moved her head back and forth slowly, as if I were crazy.

I grinned at her. "I figure the first time you were just making sure Mom took her planted friend — that would be me — along wherever she was going. I was just ducking back in the gallery to get her purse, but she'd already ditched me twice, and you thought she was ditching me again. So you gave her a little push and hoped for the best. In fact, you've been in London the whole time you pretended to be in Florida. You've got a block on your cell phone to keep your location from showing on the screen. Every time you called you were probably twenty feet away watching me."

Sunni's head was still doing that shaking thing, and her eyes were hurt and confused.

"You were the blonde in the Jackie O glasses trailing me around town the day I lost your mother. I thought it was a guy, but then I remembered how much time you spent barefoot on the beach. Heels hurt when you're out of practice.

"You were also the blonde at the gallery the night your mother collapsed, the one who handed me her purse. Nobody in the entire place knew Mrs. Russell, but you handed me her bag with complete trust. Your mom says you use men to get things done, so I figure you hustled down there and moved in on young Dmitri after I phoned you about the gallery opening. You met him there that night as his date, which was pretty fast work, but you've had a lot of experience, right? And Dmitri was probably a mine of information about Josef, Edward and the rest of them."

I stopped talking as the waiter arrived and asked if we were ready to order. I shook my head and Sunni smiled, took a solid slug of her drink and ordered another round. She switched the smile to me, and there was amusement in her voice. "I should have checked your background a little more carefully before hiring you. Does Tom know you're a whack job?"

"I just talked to Tom actually. He says you haven't been around for at least a week. Oh, and he was turned off by your Barbie doll wig, just as a point of interest. Didn't it occur to you we'd talk? Didn't you think I'd find out?"

Her eyes narrowed slightly as she shook her head. "It wouldn't occur to me you'd believe anything Tom Roddler said. Another total whack job."

I shrugged and let it go. "I couldn't figure out how you knew I was meeting your mother at the Wolseley for breakfast, but you hired a private detective over here once before, and I'm guessing you got another one to follow Mom around since I was so bad at it. Then you got rid of him, waited 'til she came out and gave her a second shove. Only this time, you meant to do more than scare her."

Sunni said in a perfectly friendly voice, "You're crazy as shit."

"The bomb was a dumb move, though. They'll ask Dmitri why it isn't at the gallery, and he'll tell when he realizes you've left him holding the bag. Is the rental car in his name too? If not, it's more than your word against his. He'll recognize you, short red hair or not. So will his gallerista girlfriend, who refers to you as the blonde American bitch. And the police in Derbyshire . . ."

"Look," she interrupted, "you've got one hell of an imagina-
tion, I'll give you that. The truth is, I did rent a car and let Dmitri
take it one afternoon, but only because he asked me to. I don't
know what he got up to while he had it. And, yes, all right, I
did fly over a couple of days before you did. I wasn't going to
tell you because I didn't want you to think I was pathetic, but
I wanted to be on the scene in case you found my dad — or
in case Mummy dearest suddenly got an overdue case of conscience and wanted to introduce me to him."

"Oh, right. The father you never knew. I can tell you about
that, but I don't think you're going to like it."

Her eyes narrowed, and for a second I was glad we were
sitting amidst a crowd of business lunchers and not somewhere
out of screaming-for-help distance.

"It's that fucking Edward, isn't it? I hate do-gooders, especially the ones who want to do good with other people's money.
You'd think she'd be smarter than that. He's been married twice
already."

"Like you?" I murmured.

She shot me a look of disgust. "I knew it was him, I had a
feeling."

"So, on the off chance that your mother might fund a few
of Edward's African wells, you pushed her in front of a bus?"

"Oh, please. My stepfather left her every cent. I have a
small trust, but it's barely enough to live on. It would all have
come to me if she stayed single, which she seemed to be doing.
But I've read the P.I. reports. I know how many times they've
shacked up and how they hang all over each other."

"So it was just about money?"

"Of course it's money. I'm not crazy, and there's a bucket
of loot involved. If it all goes into a bottomless pit in some ass-
backwards African hellhole, what good's that do anybody?"

"Still, she couldn't spend it all . . ."

"Do you know how many fucking African states there are? Darfur, Tanzania — they're just flavors of the month. She won't have a dime left." She took a breath and let it out all at once. "I never meant to *hurt* her, not ever, just scare her off."

"So you planted a ridiculous, obviously fake bomb?"

Sunni shrugged. "It was just something to try, and it was attached to his property. I figured if he thought she was enough of a liability, he'd dump her. That's what guys do. And it would have been better for her anyway. Even you should be able to see that."

I let my eyes get wider. "You were doing it for *her*?"

"You don't have to be such a jerk about it. I am her daughter, and the money did come from *my* stepfather. He wouldn't have wanted me left without anything." She moved forward in her chair. "Are we about done here? I don't have time for this shit. You really have a bang-up idea of loyalty, you know that?"

I looked at her in near admiration. "You're certainly more than the standard piece of work. I planned to do this much better, soft pedal it a little because I felt kind of sorry for you, but not now. You meant to kill or seriously injure the only living relative you've got in the world. You don't merit special handling."

I took out a folded piece of paper.

"Your mother has asked me to give you this. One, she's settled quite a large sum of money on you. Two, it starts getting deposited into your bank account — monthly — the minute you return to the U.S. Three, the deposits stop on her death, no matter what the cause. Four, she has changed her will and no other money or property will come to you. Five, she mailed a registered letter to her attorney this morning explaining what you've done. That's in case anything happens to her — or me. I didn't think it was necessary, but she knows you better than

I do. Six, she doesn't want to see you again, and if you try to contact her or any of her friends, even by accident, the monthly deposits stop. And seven, seven is mine. I'm going to tell you about your father."

I gave her his name and explained the connection.

It took a moment before she understood, and then words spewed out of her open mouth as her face turned the color of used Play Doh.

"That stupid, mother fucking asshole, that stupid mother fucker . . ."

I made no attempt to shush her, just sat back and watched. The waiter, who was within hearing distance, was regarding her in alarm, as were people from surrounding tables. When she realized it, she bit down on her tongue so hard it hurt to watch and lowered her voice to a hiss. She sounded like a snake.

"You tell her," she stuck a finger in my face, jabbing within inches of my eyes, "she won't get away with this. I'll take her to court, and by the time I'm finished dragging her through the dirt, she won't have any reputation left. Unsolved murder when she was twenty, illegal flight, impersonating a dead person, passport violations. They'll declare her incompetent — her and her fucking psychics — and the money will all come to me anyway. I'll make her sorry she's alive."

"I don't think I'd do that."

"I don't give a shit what you think." She jumped to her feet and reached under the table, but I kicked the duffle bag out of her reach.

"If I were you," I said, "I'd worry more about whether your mother legally inherits the Russell money at all — since she was married to someone else when she hooked up with your stepfather. And more especially since she isn't who he thought he was leaving it to."

I uttered the partial lie without a twinge of conscience. "It's a question of keeping quiet, keeping away from her, and keeping cash flowing into your account. Otherwise, the money will go to lawyers — the ones representing every obscure relative your stepfather ever had as soon as it hits the evening news."

I refolded the paper, slid it across to her and stood up. "This is your copy. Your monthly amount is under point number two. Much larger than you deserve. And here," I handed her an envelope, "is what you paid me for this job. I'm refunding the full amount." I got up and headed in the direction of the ladies' room.

When I returned to the terrace a few minutes later, the paper, the envelope, Sunni and her duffle bag were gone. I paid for the wine and left the waiter a large, apologetic tip. Then I called Edward, who said Susan wasn't answering her door or her phone.

"I was just about to call her." I told him. "The person who pushed her won't be doing that anymore, but you should hear the story from her. Even if she says she wants to handle it alone, I think you should insist. She's going to need you."

I disconnected and called Susan to say that I'd carried out her instructions. Her voice was listless, and she didn't ask for details. After a long silence that neither of us broke, she said thank you and she'd see me later. Then, as an afterthought in the same incurious voice, "You left some things on the dresser, Keegan, house keys it looks like, boarding pass, checkbook. Under a magazine. I'll keep them for you."

Reid met me at the elevator, and we rode down eight floors to the wharf. There was no sign of Sunni, but I kept an eye out anyway as we walked slowly along the river to London Eye.

It was too nice a day to get shoved in the Thames.

Chapter 25

It took another week for Susan Russell to ditch her cold. I visited her twice at the B&B. The first time we didn't talk much, and she looked terrible. The second time she was worse. She coughed non-stop, had trouble breathing and segued from burning fever to shuddering chills every two or three minutes. When I suggested a hospital and a team of doctors, she refused.

"It's all right, Steven says I'm just having a major de-tox."

Good old medically trained Steven.

"Just getting rid of all the old bad stuff that's been gunking up my system for years. He told me what to take, and Edward got it from the homeopathic clinic." She gestured weakly at a bedside table full of powders and bottle droppers. "He says to get outside as soon as I can, you know, bare feet on the earth, smell the rain, embrace clean green things."

I gave her a look. "He wants you to hug a tree?"

She started to giggle, but it became a hacking cough. "A whole forest, I think."

I took the small recorder out of my purse and placed it next to a bottle of vitamin C. "I was going to wait until you were better, but I may have to fly home before that happens. Do you want to hear this?"

"No. It was what we thought, wasn't it? All her — all the time?"

"Yes. At first she was trying to frighten you, make you go home, preferably without Edward. Then she realized how much easier it would be the other way."

She closed her eyes. "I never loved her completely . . . not after she got older. She was half of him, and every time she did something unethical or mean or greedy . . . she was such a greedy kid, even at two years old . . . I couldn't get past it. Maybe I caused it, made her worse. Always watching for some sign that she was going to end up like him." She opened her eyes a little and studied me through the slits. "I never asked. What did you tell Sunni about her father?"

"Who he was."

"But how could you possibly know that?"

"Partly because you left Rhode Island in such a hurry when your husband was arrested. It would have made more sense to wait around and see if they gave him ten years. And partly because you started throwing up when you learned Tony's mother was coming to stay. You were also sick when you were running away to England. Seemed like an excess of throwing up to me. Unless you were pregnant. Except Tony had a vasectomy and his mother probably knew it, so if you were expecting, you were in big trouble and wouldn't be able to hide it for long. And since you weren't allowed to go anywhere, the only guy you spent time with was the one your husband hired to keep tabs on you. Good old Earl, the Rhode Island hit man."

"He was a charmer — when he wasn't killing people." Susan managed a twisted smile and wiped her nose. "Tony and I were fighting all the time, and Earl was a hunk, blonde and tan and laid back. Always telling me how beautiful I was and how lucky Tony was and that he couldn't understand why a guy that lucky didn't treat his wife better. He was the only one telling me anything good, and eventually I believed him. The sex was . . . amazing . . . and then I couldn't stop and then I was sorry and then I was pregnant. Even then I couldn't stop."

She sighed.

"Tony would have killed me when he found out, and I didn't know what Earl would do. So I ran. I always blamed myself for Abby's death, but I see now she got there all by herself, just by being such a good hater. She hated them all: Liz for standing in her way, Nigel for vying for Josef's affections, Josef for not getting free quickly enough, Edward for disapproving of her fast and loose behavior. The only one she didn't hate was me, probably because I didn't have anything she wanted. Except clothes."

She smiled at me through dark rimmed, exhausted eyes.

"They always joked that if you could remember London in the Sixties, you weren't there; but I remember it all, every color, every smell, every cold, raw day."

"Susan," I said gently, "you were only here six months or so."

Her mouth opened and forgot to close. The look of shock that replaced the exhausted look was almost comical.

"You're right, you're exactly right." She struggled to sit up against her pillows. "I operated in a kind of fog for years trying to pay somehow for bringing evil on my friends. Weeding the corn and beans, wearing smelly moccasins I made myself, baking thirty loaves of bread every morning. Working off all that bad karma — doing penance for those months of mistakes. Well, nine months, given the circumstances."

She shook her head. "When we left the commune, I thought I'd done my time and could start over clean. But it's hard when you're still keeping secrets. I didn't do a good job with my daughter. I couldn't tell anybody, let alone Sunni, that her father was a hit man. Maybe if I'd gotten help sooner or tried harder —"

"Maybe you're taking too much credit. Maybe she was just a really hard person to love."

She nodded slowly, then reached out her hand for the recorder. "I think I want this after all. I'll put it in the safe deposit box, just in case. But I'm not going to listen to it."

I nodded. "Good idea."

Five days later, around three in the afternoon, I went to meet Susan Russell at the Victoria Embankment. The sun was glorious, and a couple dozen boats were churning up and down the blue and glittering Thames as if they owned it.

When a slender woman, hair more blonde than red, with glowing skin and green eyes came walking toward me, I looked past her before I realized it was Mrs. Russell. She was wearing knee length khaki shorts, a black T-shirt and black running shoes, and she looked more my age than her own. A back pack was looped over one arm.

I shook my head. "Good God, I can't believe it. You look terrific."

She grinned at me. "Great stuff, homeopathics. That and unloading forty years of crap."

"I guess so. Cold completely gone?"

"Absolutely. Even the bruises." She moved the back pack to her other arm. "Want to walk for a while?"

We strolled up the sidewalk past people sitting on park benches and children running ahead of their parents. There was plenty of traffic coming off Waterloo Bridge, but the noise it made was more background than intrusive.

"I've done a lot of mental house cleaning the last few days," Susan was saying, "and I've finally realized that every morning you get up you're dealing with a different body, mind and place in time." She paused. "That's important because I've spent most of my life living in the past. I was brought up on my mother's England — the Thirties and Forties — and when I got here in 1966, it hadn't really changed. It seemed different because of the Beatles and free love and miniskirts, but men still wore suits and bowler hats to work and carried furled umbrellas. You still went to the butcher for meat and the fishmonger for sole and the greengrocer for lettuce and peas. Hamburgers came topped with fried eggs and mounds of chips, money was shillings and thruppences and and ha' pennies, Lyons Corner Houses had good tea and bad food, and when you bought a newspaper for six pence, they always said, 'Ta, love.' "

She drew in a breath. "My mother's London is gone and so is mine. Starbucks on every corner, cell phones stuck in every ear. It's just like any big city anywhere."

"True." I grinned at her. "My England was the late Eighties and early Nineties, and there's not a lot left of it either. So, what are you going to do now?"

"I'm staying with Edward for the moment. We've applied for visas for Africa, and we're going to check out his wells." She rolled her eyes at me. "Sunni's worst nightmare. I think he and I might work out this time around, but it doesn't really matter. Detaching from outcome — one of Stephen's biggest lessons. I'm not thinking much beyond that."

"You might have lunch with Nigel," I suggested. "I hope you

don't mind, but I called him the night Liz confessed. I thought
he deserved to know."

"Actually, I'm meeting him tonight for dinner, just the two
of us. I had coffee with Josef this morning, and we put the gallery business to rest. Closure all over the place." She cocked her
head to one side and smiled at me. "Just for my own information, did you return the retainer my daughter gave you?"

"I had to. I didn't help her."

She nodded. "I figured. What are your plans now, Keegan?"

"I'm sticking around for a while. Reid and I are taking the
Chunnel to Paris on Tuesday and spending a couple of nights
at a hotel he likes. We'll drink some really good wine, eat steak
and frites, maybe go look at Jim Morrison's grave in La Pere La
Chaise. You know, The Doors?"

"Sounds good." Her eyes moved to look over the river.
"You really have been my . . ." her voice wavered, then stead-
ied, "guardian angel, and there's no way to adequately repay
you. I do, however, have a lot of money . . ."

I could feel my head shaking no and wondered what the hell
my head thought it was doing. Of course she could give me
money if she wanted to. It was going to take forever to pay
off my VISA card. My mouth had no more sense than my
head. What came out of it was, "No, thanks for thinking of
it, but . . . no."

Susan Miachi Russell reached out, slipped both arms around
me and hugged me for longer than either of us was probably
comfortable with. "Then take care. I'll probably see you again
someday. You never know."

"I'll watch for you and Edward on the cover of *Time*."

She smiled at me a second longer, turned to go, then
reached back and handed me the backpack. "Almost forgot. A
very small thank you." She waved at a taxi, it swerved over to

pick her up, and with another wave she was gone. Just like the day I followed her along the King's Road.

I crossed the street at the next light, stopped at an outdoor café and ordered a Diet Coke before I unzipped the backpack. Inside was a Nikon D90 with a 70-30 telephoto lens and two SD chips. There was also an envelope with fifteen one hundred dollar bills and a note:

> I knew you'd give back Sunni's money, so please use this to cover your expenses. Also, I watched your face at Edward's the night you were cleaning the cameras — and I don't think you're finished with photography yet. If you are, you can hock this; if not, as the English say — it's always best to begin as you mean to go along. It is, for our sins, a digital world. Bless you, Keegan.

When the girl came with my Coke, I was breathing again, but tears were still sliding out the corners of my eyes onto the zoom lens.

I returned to Seminole Beach almost a month later than I'd intended. The tenants had not burned down or otherwise destroyed the house, and no one had visible black and blue marks. Amy, who was again cooking full time, served baked lobster for my welcome back dinner.

Ten days after I got home, Reid called to ask if he could visit for a couple of weeks in November. We've fixed up one of the empty rooms for him — the one closest to mine.

Two weeks after that, a letter came from my bank saying $25,000 had been deposited into my account from the Russell Foundation in payment for consultation services and five more installments of specified amounts would be made over the next three years. The total amount was staggering.

For a moment I couldn't understand how she'd managed to get my account numbers. Then I remembered the night I'd gone to Lewes to see Liz and the items I'd removed from my bag to make room for Edward's brandy. One of those items had been the checkbook Mrs. Russell had found and returned to me along with my keys.

Evidently she'd been planning it even then.

About the Author

Sandra J. Robson is a speech pathologist and the author of a mystery novel, *False Impression*, and a self-help book, *Girls' Night Out: Changing Your Life One Week at a Time*. She has lived in London and traveled extensively in the British Isles. She resides on the east coast of Florida with her orthodontist husband.

Visit Sandra's website at www.SandraRobson.com.